LUCY IN THE SKY

LUCY IN THE SKY

Written by

Kiara Brinkman

Art by

Sean Chiki

:01

First Second

New York

1. LUCY SUTCLIFFE
2. VANESSA TAKAHASHI
3. GEORGIANNA BIRK
4. RUPA KHANNA
5. KATE
6. RYAN
7. CONNOR
8. PETE
9. ISABEL TRANTON
10. DANIEL SUTCLIFFE
11. ELEANOR "COOKIE" TRANTON
12. EMILY
13. MR. DOYLE
14. MAYA
15. MRS. TAKAHASHI
16. CAMILLE
17. MR. KHANNA
18. MRS. KHANNA
19. MRS. SCOTT
20. MR. TAKAHASHI

Text © 2021 by Kiara Brinkman
Illustration © 2021 by Sean Chiki
Published by First Second, an imprint of Roaring Brook
Press, a division of Holtzbrinck Publishing Holdings Limited
Partnership. 120 Broadway, New York, NY 10271.
All rights reserved.
Library of Congress Control Number: 2019947778
First edition, 2021. Edited by Calista Brill and Robyn
Chapman. Cover design by Kirk Benshoff. Interior book
design by Molly Johanson. Special thanks to Sarah Myer.
Printed in China by 1010 Printing International Ltd.,
North Point, Hong Kong.
Penciled with a Pentel Graph Gear 500 mechanical pencil with 0.5
HB lead on Strathmore drawing paper. Traced onto Strathmore
bristol board with an Artograph LightPad. Inked with a Hunt 56
dip pen and Winsor & Newton calligraphy ink. Lettered with a
Pigma Micron 08 pen. Colored digitally in Photoshop.
Our books may be purchased in bulk for promotional,
educational, or business use. Please contact your local
bookseller or the Macmillan Corporate and Premium Sales
Department at MacmillanSpecialMarkets@macmillan.com.
Paperback ISBN: 978-1-62672-720-5
Hardcover ISBN: 978-1-62672-721-2
Paperback: 10 9 8 7 6 5 4 3 2 1
Hardcover: 10 9 8 7 6 5 4 3 2 1
Don't miss your next favorite book from First Second!
For the latest updates go to firstsecondnewsletter.com and
sign up for our enewsletter.

fall 2012

OH, HEY.

WHAT'S UP?

YOU'RE SO LUCKY YOU'RE NOT IN ALGEBRA.

YEAH. MR. ROSSI SMELLS LIKE A COMBINATION OF COFFEE AND COUGH DROPS, AND BY THE END OF THE DAY, HIS WHOLE BACK IS TOTALLY COVERED IN CHALK.

IT'S SO DEPRESSING.

CRAP. I HAVE PIANO IN LIKE FIFTEEN MINUTES!

SEE YA!

ARE YOU GOING TO YOUR GRANDMA'S?

NO.

I WAS JUST GOING TO WALK OVER TO THE MUSIC STO—

RIGHT...

IT'S TUESDAY.

TELL ME YOU'RE NOT GOING TO BUY THE NEW ONE 4 ALL.

...

DID YOU SEE THAT NEW MISS DEED VIDEO ON YOUTUBE?

EXCUSE ME.

FOR MY KID.

$18.95.

SHE'S IN THE FOURTH GRADE.

DO YOU WANT A BAG FOR THAT?

OF COURSE WE CAN'T JUST DOWNLOAD THE THING FOR $9.99 ON iTUNES, BECAUSE THE CD SUPPOSEDLY COMES WITH A FOLD-OUT POSTER. WHAT DOES THAT MAKE IT—A TEN-DOLLAR POSTER?

A NINE-DOLLAR POSTER.

YOU WANT A BAG FOR THAT?

YOU'RE FEELING OKAY?

MUCH BETTER.

YOU'RE STILL COMING FOR DINNER TOMORROW, RIGHT?

OF COURSE. I THOUGHT I'D MAKE A BATCH OF SNICKERDOODLES FOR DESSERT. BUT YOU KNOW WHAT...

I THINK MY TREATMENT'S RUINING MY SWEET TOOTH.

THAT'S IMPOSSIBLE!

NO, IT'S TRUE...

... MY TASTEBUDS ARE INDIFFERENT.

HUH.

OH, MY POOR FERN.

COME ON, LITTLE FELLOW, PERK UP!

DID YOU SEE THE NEW ISSUE OF *WORLD TRAVELER?*

NOT YET... WHERE'S YOUR MOTHER BEEN TO NOW?

TONGA!

STANDING ON TOP OF A VOLCANO, I BET.

PRETTY MUCH.

THAT CHILD WAS INCORRIGIBLE FROM THE BEGINNING. THREE YEARS OLD AND I FIND THAT SHE'S CLIMBED OUT HER BEDROOM WINDOW TO PLAY ON THE ROOF!

I WONDER WHAT SHE SENT ME. DO YOU THINK THEY SELL SNOW GLOBES IN TONGA?

IT'S A LITTLE LATE FOR A SNACK, LUCE.

I'M MAKING FALAFEL TONIGHT.

THINK OF THIS AS MY APPETIZER.

DID YOU FIGURE OUT WHAT YOU WANT TO DO FOR YOUR BIRTHDAY?

PROBABLY JUST A SLEEPOVER.

WITH VANESSA AND RUPA?

YEAH.

WELL, LET ME KNOW IF YOU WANT ME TO PICK UP ANYTHING SPECIAL... WE COULD MAKE A PIZZA AGAIN LIKE LAST YEAR.

YOU OKAY?

(SIGH) YEAH.

?

I HAVE TO DO MY HOMEWORK.

20

BUT WHAT IF YOU WANTED TO WORK WITH YOUR DAD AT THE PARLOR?

TOO DANGEROUS FOR A GIRL, ACCORDING TO MY MOTHER.

EVEN THOUGH NOBODY EVER BOTHERS ROBBING ICE CREAM SHOPS, SHE'S PARANOID.

ANYWAY, I'D LOOK TERRIBLE IN THE HAT.

2 FLAVORS

MY OLDEST COUSIN, ARUN, IS SET TO TAKE OVER WHEN MY DAD RETIRES.

I JUST NEED TO PRACTICE THE MIDDLE SECTION.

I DON'T KNOW HOW TO EXPLAIN...

IT'S LIKE MY MOM'S ALWAYS SAYING...

"LOOK AT ME, I HAVE BAGS UNDER MY EYES."

"I AM SO TIRED WHEN I DRIVE HOME FROM WORK THAT I HAVE TO PINCH MY CHEEKS TO STAY AWAKE. YOU DON'T WANT TO BE A NURSE LIKE ME."

AND IT JUST GOES WITHOUT SAYING THAT BEING A DOCTOR IS THE ONLY OTHER OPTION.

I GOTTA RUN.

SEE YA!

GOOD LUCK AT THE RECITAL!

ORCHESTRA ROOM

BOOM TIK BUM TIK BO

IN ONE OF THE BOXES IN THE HALLWAY CLOSET UPSTAIRS. CAN I GET IT FOR YOU LATER?

NO!

OLD TOYS

X-MAS LIGHTS

HERE YOU GO.

WHAT'S IN THIS BOX ANYWAY? IT'S SO HEAVY!

THEY'RE RECORDS. MY OLD COLLECTION.

AND SOME OF YOUR MOM'S, TOO.

HANG ON.

THANKS.

THAT'S THE PASTA.

BE EEP

IF COOKIE'S NOT HERE BY 7:30, WE'LL GIVE HER A CALL.

TOYS
LUCY BABY CLOTHES
STER
HALLOWEEN STUFF
DANIEL LINENS
LUCY LINENS

THEY LOOK SO...

introd
THE BEATLES
ENGLAND's No.1 VOCAL GROUP

KIND.

!

[V₆J]
TRODUCING THE BEATLES
SIDE ONE
SAW HER
SIDE TWO
PLEASE PLEASE

4ALL

YEAH.

LIKE THEY'D HELP AN OLD LADY SAFELY CROSS THE STREET.

[V₆J]

BUT ACTUALLY, AT THE TIME, PEOPLE THOUGHT THEY LOOKED REALLY STRANGE.

?

[V₆J]
INTRODUCING THE BEATLES

REALLY. THEIR HAIRCUTS...

I LIKE HIM.

HE'S JUST, LIKE, GOOFY.

GOOD OLD RINGO— NOT THE MOST WELL-LOVED BEATLE.

[Vd] INTRODUCING THE BEATLES

[Vd]

WELL, HE'S MY FAVORITE!

OKAY, LADIES, TIME TO EAT!

WHICH ONE DO YOU LIKE THE BEST?

[Vd] 'CING THE BEATLES

SWEET GEORGE.

HOW DO YOU EVEN PLAY THIS THING?

I'LL SHOW YOU AFTER DINNER.

DOES MOM HAVE A FAVORITE BEATLE?

JOHN, OF COURSE.

THE LOOSE CANNON.

OF COURSE.

I'VE ALWAYS BEEN A PAUL GUY.

THE ETERNAL ROMANTIC.

CHUCKLE

[Vd] INTRODUCING THE BEATLES

WHAT?

"LP" (LONG-PLAYING) RECORDS ARE 12 INCHES WIDE AND PLAY AT $33\frac{1}{3}$ RPM (REVOLUTIONS PER MINUTE).

ADAPTOR USED FOR SINGLE'S CENTER HOLE.

"SINGLES" ARE 7 INCHES AND PLAY AT 45 RPM.

MGM
45

45 SINGLE

THERE ARE ALSO "EP" (EXTENDED-PLAY) RECORDS, WHICH CONTAIN MORE SONGS THAN A SINGLE, BUT NOT AS MANY AS AN LP. AN EP MAY PLAY AT $33\frac{1}{3}$ RPM OR AT 45 RPM. SOME OLDER RECORDS ARE CALLED 78S, BECAUSE THEY PLAY AT 78 RPM.

HOW TO PLAY A
PHONOGRAPH
RECORD

UNTIL THE 1960S, MOST POP MUSIC WAS PRODUCED IN MONOPHONIC (MONO) SOUND, MEANT TO BE PLAYED THROUGH ONE SPEAKER. BY THE LATE '60S STEREOPHONIC SOUND (STEREO), WHICH MADE USE OF TWO SPEAKERS, BECAME DOMINANT.

VIDEO
CD PHONO
L
R

IF NEEDED, PLUG YOUR TURNTABLE INTO AN AMPLIFIER OR RECEIVER.

FOR STEREO RECORDINGS, PLACE YOUR SPEAKERS FAR ENOUGH APART TO ACHIEVE OPTIMUM STEREO EFFECT.

NOW YOU'RE READY TO PLAY A PHONOGRAPH RECORD!

WHY IS IT THAT HANDCLAPS MAKE A SONG INFINITELY BETTER?

ARE YOU OKAY?

A LITTLE TUCKERED OUT.

LET ME GET YOU SOME WATER.

I DON'T THINK I'M A VERY GOOD DANCER.

YOU'RE THINKING ABOUT IT TOO MUCH.

DANCING IS ABOUT FORGETTING.

BUT IF I PLAY THE DRUMS LIKE RINGO, THEN I WON'T HAVE TO DANCE AT ALL.

I SUPPOSE THAT'S TRUE.

I WISH I HAD MY OWN KIT, SO I COULD REALLY PRACTICE.

CAN I DRIVE YOU HOME?

WE HAVEN'T HAD DESSERT YET!

LUCY...

THE SNICKERDOODLES ARE IN THE TUPPERWARE.

KISS

I THINK I SET THEM ON THE COUNTER NEXT TO THE FRIDGE.

YOU HAVE AN EXTRA ONE FOR ME.

OKAY?

SKRTCHH ...

MISERY!...

TAP TAP

TAP TAP

MRS. SCOTT SHOULD BRING IN A MALE MODEL.

THAT WOULD BE MORE INTERESTING THAN A TRICYCLE.

ANYWAAAY...

MRS. SCOTT GOES ON THIS RANT ABOUT MELTING GLACIERS...

... AND HOW ALL THE BIRDS IN TOWN HAVE NO IDEA WHAT SEASON IT IS OR WHETHER TO MIGRATE...

... BUT IT'S LIKE SHE'S ANGRY AT US, PERSONALLY, LIKE WE'VE CAUSED GLOBAL WARMING...

SHE HAD TO PRACTICALLY CHUG HER CHAMOMILE TEA TO CALM HERSELF DOWN.

BY THE END OF CLASS, SHE WAS HER NORMAL, PEACEFUL, HAPPY SELF AGAIN.

LA, LA, LA, LA!

THEY SHOULD REALLY TURN THE AIR-CONDITIONING BACK ON.

MY MOM CALLED AND COMPLAINED ABOUT IT...

YOU KNOW, MAYBE IF WE ALL STARTED FAINTING FROM HEAT EXHAUSTION THEY'D TAKE US SERIOUSLY.

SPEAKING OF WHICH, IN PE, LAUREN WANG TOLD ME THAT SHE HAS TOTALLY CONQUERED HER STAGE FRIGHT AND SHE'S ALREADY PRACTICING FOR THE TALENT SHOW.

SHE'S PASSED OUT MID SONG THREE YEARS IN A ROW NOW. TIME TO ACCEPT THAT FAINTING IS HER SPECIAL TALENT.

" NOT IN MY CASTLE ON A CLOU... "

YOU'RE SO MEAN.

I'VE BEEN PRACTICING ON MY KARAOKE MACHINE.

FEEL THE GREED WHEN YOU'RE IN NEED. COME ON AND DO THE DEED.

KEEP PRACTICING.

HEY!

MUNCH MUNCH

IS YOUR MOM GOING TO MAKE YOU PLAY A TEN-MINUTE SONATA AGAIN?

ZZZZ

HA HA HA HA

NO.

I'LL THREATEN TO PERMANENTLY GO ON STRIKE! MY COUSIN QUIT PIANO TWO YEARS AGO, AND MY AUNTIE STILL HASN'T RECOVERED.

I WONDER HOW GEORGIANNA WILL FOLLOW UP LAST YEAR'S DISASTER.

I THOUGHT IT WAS COOL...

"CALL ME MAYBE" JUST DOESN'T WORK ON ACOUSTIC GUITAR.

SHE, LIKE, ZAPPED ALL THE LIFE OUT OF IT.

THAT WAS KIND OF THE POINT.

TO SLOW DOWN A GOOD SONG BEYOND RECOGNITION AND BE TRAGICALLY DEPRESSING?

YEAH, BECAUSE IF YOU THINK ABOUT IT, THE LYRICS ARE WEIRDLY DESPERATE AND SAD.

WHAT, ARE YOU TWO THE ONLY MEMBERS OF SOME SECRET GEORGIANNA BIRK FAN CLUB?

YOU BETTER HOPE SHE DOESN'T FIND OUT THAT YOU LISTEN TO ONE FOR ALL, BECAUSE SHE'S A TOTAL SNOB.

I DON'T LISTEN TO THEM ANYMORE.

SINCE WHEN?

A PERSON CAN CHANGE.

... BUT THE MOUTH OF A WISE MAN IS IN HIS HEART.

AYE, AYE!

SO, DO YOU WANNA MAKE PIZZA TONIGHT WITH THE GIRLS?

CAN WE GO OUT TO DINNER?

SURE, IT'S YOUR DAY. WHERE TO?

UMAMI!

!

BUT YOU DON'T LIKE SUSHI.

I DIDN'T LIKE IT WHEN I WAS LITTLE.

I HAVEN'T TRIED IT SINCE MOM LEFT.

OKAY, THEN, SUSHI IT IS!

MOM'S NOT COMING BACK, Y'KNOW.

I'M STILL SUPPOSED TO WEAR MY RETAINER AT NIGHT. I DON'T EVEN KNOW WHERE THE STUPID THING IS.

I SWEAR, SINCE I GOT MY BRACES OFF, MY MOM IS OBSESSED WITH MY TEETH.

SHE JUST COMES UP TO ME AND TELLS ME TO SMILE, AND THEN SHE'S TOTALLY AMAZED—

LIKE, LOOK WHAT MONEY CAN BUY!

I BET YOU DON'T HAVE A SINGLE CAVITY.

WHAT CAN I SAY, I WAS BORN WITH STRONG TEETH...

PERFECT TEETH.

MY GRANDMA HAS EATEN SWEETS FOR PROBABLY MORE THAN SIXTY YEARS AND NO CAVITIES...

IT MUST BE IN MY GENES OR SOMETHING.

NOW MY MOM SAYS GOOD NIGHT.

GOOD NIGHT, MRS. KHANNA! SLEEP TIGHT, DON'T LET THE BED BUGS BITE!

HA HA HA HA HA HA HA HA HA

YOU KNOW, YOUR DAD'S KIND OF COOL.

I MEAN, RELATIVELY SPEAKING.

NO, HE'S NOT!

DORKY COOL.

NO WAY!

MRS. KHANNA, IF YOU'RE STILL AWAKE, RUPA HAS A CRUSH ON LUCY'S DAD!

!

45

AT LEAST I DON'T HAVE A CRUSH ON THE SCHOOL LIBRARIAN!

FOR THE MILLIONTH TIME, I THINK HE'S NICE — THAT'S ALL.

OH MY GOD, I JUST HAD THE BEST REALIZATION!

WHAT ?!

WE COULD TOTALLY BE A BAND.

DRUMS.

KEYBOARD.

VOICE.

BUT I DON'T HAVE A KEYBOARD...

WE'LL GET YOU ONE.

UM, I THINK WE'RE ALSO GONNA NEED A GUITAR PLAYER.

GEORGIANNA BIRK !

RIGHT, SO WHO'S GONNA ASK HER?

...IT WON'T BE LONG. YEAH!

YEAH!...

YEAH!...

YEAH!...

YEAH!...

YEAH!

46

DON'T WE ALSO NEED A BASS PLAYER?

DAD!

MR. SUTCLIFFE'S GONNA BE OUR BASS PLAYER.

GIGGLE

EVERYTHING OKAY?

CAN WE HAVE A BAND WITHOUT A BASS PLAYER?

SURE, WHY NOT? THE DOORS WERE JUST DRUMS, GUITAR, AND KEYBOARD. RAY MANZAREK COULD MAKE HIS KEYBOARD SOUND LIKE A BASS.

RAY WHO?

RAY MANZAREK...

JIM MORRISON...

"BREAK ON THROUGH TO THE OTHER SIDE"...

"LIGHT MY FIRE"...

OH, YEAH.

AND THE WHITE STRIPES WERE A DUO— GUITAR AND DRUMS.

YOU LISTEN TO THE WHITE STRIPES?

WELL, I'M AWARE OF THEM.

HE READS MUSIC MAGAZINES.

SO WE'RE ALL SET!

EXCEPT I HAVE TO LEARN HOW TO PLAY THE DRUMS...

EXPECTING A MESSAGE FROM YOUR BOYFRIEND?

HE'S NOT MY BOYFRIEND!

IT'S NOT OFFICIAL ON FACEBOOK OR ANYTHING. WE'RE JUST GOING OUT.

SO WHERE D'YOU GO OUT?

NOWHERE YET.

I'LL TALK TO GEORGIANNA.

YEAH RIGHT.

I WILL!

LOOK, WE'RE GOING TO THE SAME PLACE, SO WE MIGHT AS WELL WALK TOGETHER.

SEE YOU LATER.

I LOVE BEN FRANKLIN.

ME, TOO! HE'S BEEN SITTING THERE EVER SINCE I CAN REMEMBER.

YEAH.

HEY, GEORGIE.

WHAT'S UP, PETE?

GOOD NEWS.

WE JUST GOT IN A 7-INCH OF "DESDEMONA."

THAT'S NOT GOOD NEWS, THAT'S CRAZY-EXCELLENT-AMAZING NEWS!

I'M A TINY BIT OBSESSED WITH MARC BOLAN.

?

OH, UH, PETE, THIS IS LUCY— LUCY, PETE.

SO, WHERE IS IT?!

WITH T. REX.

YOU JUST PUT IT OUT?

WHAT IF SOMEONE ELSE FOUND IT FIRST?

THEM'S THE BREAKS.

ANYWAY, IT SHOULDN'T BE WITH T. REX...

NOBODY'S EVER HEARD OF HIS FIRST BAND...

JOHN'S CHILDREN.

RIGHT. NOBODY EXCEPT YOU.

SO YOU JUST CATER TO THE MASSES?

THAT'S MY JOB!

?

TEN DOLLARS!

FOR A 7-INCH?

IT'S IN *PERFECT* CONDITION.

NOW I DON'T HAVE ENOUGH MONEY FOR THE CAT POWER.

I'VE BEEN WANTING IT FOR WEEKS AND EVERY TIME I THINK I'M GOING TO BUY IT, I GET LURED BY SOMETHING ELSE.

YOU MEAN NEW MUSIC STILL COMES OUT ON RECORD?

ONLY SOME — THE GOOD STUFF.

I DIDN'T KNOW THAT GUY COULD, LIKE, ACTUALLY COMMUNICATE.

YEAH, HE'S A HYBRID—

HALF HUMAN, HALF ROBOT.

HIS UNCLE, WHO OWNS THE STORE, IS A COMPLETE ROBOT.

I DON'T KNOW WHAT IT IS, BUT IT SMELLS STRANGELY GOOD IN THIS LITTLE ROOM.

DUST AND STALE SUNLIGHT.

ROCK

SO, WHAT DO YOU LISTEN TO?

OH, UMMM, LATELY, THE BEATLES, THE EARLY ALBUMS.

MY BROTHER SAYS THERE ARE TWO KINDS OF PEOPLE IN THE WORLD—

THOSE WHO PREFER THE BEATLES AND THOSE WHO PREFER THE STONES.

WHICH KIND OF PERSON ARE YOU?

NEITHER. OR, I GUESS, BOTH. I MEAN, HOW COULD I CHOOSE BETWEEN THE BEATLES AND THE STONES?

MY BROTHER'S ALWAYS TRYING TO IMPOSE HIS OWN WEIRD SENSE OF ORDER ON THE WORLD.

MISC. ROCK A - C

ADAM ANT

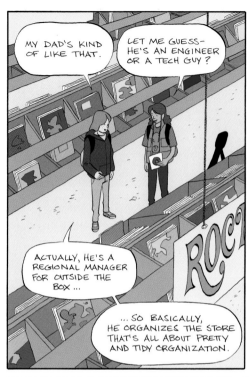

MY DAD'S KIND OF LIKE THAT.

LET ME GUESS— HE'S AN ENGINEER OR A TECH GUY?

ACTUALLY, HE'S A REGIONAL MANAGER FOR OUTSIDE THE BOX ...

... SO BASICALLY, HE ORGANIZES THE STORE THAT'S ALL ABOUT PRETTY AND TIDY ORGANIZATION.

HA HA HA HA HA HA HA HA HA HA HA

?

WHENEVER I'M IN THAT STORE, I FEEL INSPIRED TO PACK MY LIFE INTO COLORFUL, STACKABLE BOXES, BUT THEN I LEAVE, AND IT'S LIKE, *POOF,* THE INSPIRATION'S GONE.

YEAH, I HAVE TO KEEP MY EYE ON MY DAD OR EVERYTHING IN OUR HOUSE GETS PUT AWAY AND LABELED.

ARE YOU GOING TO BUY ANYTHING?

NO, I ... FORGOT MY WALLET.

WAIT!

WELL, IF HE EMERGES FROM THE DEPTHS, TELL HIM I SAY HI.

OKAY. SEE YA.

I BETTER HEAD HOME.

YEAH.

BYE.

BYE.

KNOCK

KNOCK

WHO'RE YOU?

I'M ELEANOR'S FRIEND, RUTH.

COOKIE?!

SHE'S UPSTAIRS, RESTING.

YOU'RE LUCY?

IS SHE ALL RIGHT?

THE SECOND DAY AFTER TREATMENT IS ALWAYS ROUGH.

I FORGOT...

SHOULD WE GO SEE IF SHE'S AWAKE?

I THOUGHT I HEARD YOUR VOICE.

IS EVERYTHING OKAY, BUNNY?

I JUST...

ARE YOU...

I'M FEELING KIND OF QUEASY, BUT HANGING IN THERE.

I TELL YOU WHAT, WHY DON'T YOU DO ME A HUGE FAVOR AND WATER MY PLANTS WHILE I HAVE RUTH HELP ME GET A LITTLE MORE PRESENTABLE?

THEN I'LL COME DOWN AND YOU CAN TELL ME ABOUT YOUR DAY, WHICH I'M SURE WAS MUCH MORE INTERESTING THAN MINE.

WHY DIDN'T YOU CALL ME LAST NIGHT?

I WAS BUSY...

COOKIE...

I SENT YOU, LIKE, FORTY-SEVEN TEXTS.

WHAT'S WRONG?

NOTHING. I ...

SHE SAID NO, DIDN'T SHE?

WHO?

GEORGIANNA!

SHE SAID SHE'D PRACTICE WITH US. SATURDAY AT NOON ...

THIS SATURDAY?!

CLANG

RRRRRRIIIIIIIIINNNNGGG

I DON'T EVEN HAVE A KEYBOARD YET!

I THOUGHT YOU SAID THAT THE FAMILY YOU BABYSIT FOR HAD ONE YOU COULD BORROW?

YEAH, BUT I HAVEN'T HAD A CHANCE TO...

WHAT'RE WE GOING TO PRACTICE IF WE DON'T HAVE ANY SONGS?

I DON'T KNOW.

WE'RE SO NOT READY FOR THIS!

WE'LL NEVER BE READY!

I'D LIKE TO RENEW THIS, PLEASE.

MADELINE L'ENGLE A WRINKLE

AGAIN!

GIGGLE

I SHOULD JUST BUY IT FOR YOU.

THAT WOULD BE NICE.

HOW ABOUT A PIECE OF GUM INSTEAD?

THANK YOU.

THIS WAS COOKIE'S FAVORITE SONG WHEN IT CAME OUT.

YOUR GRANDMA'S GOT GOOD TASTE.

I KNOW IT WAS HARD FOR YOU TO SEE HER LIKE THAT YESTERDAY...

I DON'T WANT TO TALK ABOUT IT.

ALL RIGHT.

I JUST WISH THINGS COULD GO BACK TO HOW THEY WERE A YEAR AGO. OR, LIKE, THREE YEARS AGO.

YEAH—LIFE GETS COMPLICATED, DOESN'T IT?

D'YOU LIKE T. REX?

THE BAND?

NO, THE DINOSAUR.

YEAH, I GUESS I APPRECIATED MARC BOLAN, BUT I ALWAYS LIKED BOWIE MORE.

WHY?

I DON'T KNOW.

HE'S SUCH A GREAT SHOWMAN, AND FOR THIRTY YEARS — NO, FORTY YEARS!...

...HE'S BEEN THIS NIMBLE CHAMELEON, CONSTANTLY TRANSFORMING INTO SOMETHING NEW.

I THINK YOUR MOM HAD A COUPLE OF T. REX ALBUMS.

SHE DID?

YOU'LL HAVE TO ASK HER.

SK RRR KUUH

ASK ME ABOUT BIO DIESEL

68

HEY.

HI.

VROOM

ASK ME ABOUT BIO-DIESEL

ASK ME

WHAT'S BIODIESEL?

BASICALLY, THE CAR RUNS ON GREASE. MY PARENTS THINK THEY'RE IN CHARGE OF SAVING THE PLANET.

OH. THAT'S COOL.

WELL, VANESSA AND RUPA SHOULD BE HERE ANY MINUTE.

DO YOU WANT A DRINK OR A SNACK OR SOMETHING? WE CAN GO INSIDE.

NAH, I'M GOOD.

WHAT'RE THOSE?

THIS ONE'S MY OVERDRIVE, AND THIS IS A PHASE SHIFTER.

?

AM I LATE?

WHAT THE *HECK* IS THAT?

MY KARAOKE MACHINE— IT'S THE ONLY MICROPHONE I HAVE.

IT'S NOT GOING TO BE LOUD ENOUGH.

AT ALL.

WE'LL JUST HAVE TO TURN DOWN.

CAN YOU PLAY WITH BRUSHES?

I CAN TRY.

I BROUGHT COOKIES.

RUPA'S NOT HERE?

NICE LUNCHBOX.

70

THANKS.

I'LL TEXT RUPA TO SEE WHAT'S GOING ON...

I DIDN'T KNOW THIS WAS A **DRESS REHEARSAL.**

AND **YOU'RE** ONE TO GIVE FASHION TIPS?

SHE'LL BE HERE IN A SEC. I GUESS SHE AND HER MOM HAD TO VISIT HER AUNT.

I DIDN'T HAVE BREAKFAST THIS MORNING.

DON'T YOU KNOW IT'S RUDE TO WATCH SOMEONE EAT?

HAVE ONE— THEY'RE YOUR FAVORITE.

!

SORRY I'M LATE. FAMILY CRISIS.

HAVE A COOKIE.

NO, NO, I JUST ATE ABOUT A THOUSAND GULAB JAMUNS AT MY AUNTIE'S. MY COUSIN HAS TO TAKE THE SAT AGAIN. HE MAY NOT BE ABLE TO MAKE THE EARLY ACTION DEADLINE FOR YALE.

HIS LIFE IS OVER.

(CHUCKLE) PRETTY MUCH. OKAY, SO I'VE HAD, LIKE, TWO SECONDS TO PLAY AROUND WITH THIS THING.

YOU DON'T HAVE AN AMP?

THIS HAS SPEAKERS.

SO FIRST ORDER OF BUSINESS — OUR NAME SUCKS.

WE HAVE A NAME?

YEAH, I TOLD YOU...

I LIKE STRAWBERRY JAM.

IT WAS JUST THE FIRST THING I THOUGHT OF... I DIDN'T...

WHAT'S WRONG WITH IT?

WELL, FOR ONE THING, STRAWBERRY JAM IS A HAMSTER.

MY HAMSTER...

HE COULD BE OUR FUZZY LITTLE MASCOT!

RUPA!

WHAT?

WE SHOULD VOTE ON IT.

BUT LUCY WASN'T EVEN SERIOUS WHEN SHE CAME UP WITH IT — SHE JUST SAID...

RRRRR...

HOW'S IT GOING?

FINE.

CUPCAKES?

(SIGH) NO, WE'RE FINE. PLEASE, DAD, JUST...

OKAY, OKAY.

LOOK, I SAY WE FORGET ABOUT THE NAME THING FOR NOW.

I SECOND THAT.

AGREED.

WHATEVER.

CAN YOU START US OFF?

NOW WHAT?

WE PLAY.

I'M REALLY ONLY GOOD AT THIS ONE BEAT.

TINGTINGTINGTINGTINGTINGTINGTIN

BOOMBOOMBAM ... BOOMBOOMBAM

RIIING

HELLO?

YEAH, HI.

SO HOW'RE THINGS?

GOOD, GOOD.

WE'RE BOTH DOING REALLY WELL.

DID YOU GET MY EMAIL?

OKAY, SURE.

SHE'S HERE—

IT'S BEEN A LONG DAY...

SHE'S...

I'M AWAKE!

JUST A SECOND.

HI, MOM.

HI, KIDDO. BIG DAY, HUH?

YEAH, BAND PRACTICE. WE DON'T HAVE HALF THE EQUIPMENT WE NEED, OR A NAME, OR, LIKE, ANYTHING, AND VANESSA...

SIGH

IS OUR VANESSA BEING A WEE BIT MELODRAMATIC?

SHE'S DRIVING ME CRAZY.

WELL, JUST LET HER KNOW SHE'S APPRECIATED. IT MAY TAKE SOME TIME FOR EVERYONE TO MESH. TRY TO HANG IN THERE.

I ONLY KNOW ONE BEAT... I HAVE TO PRACTICE SO MUCH MORE.

OKAY, SO YOU WILL, BUT KIDDO, YOU'RE GOING TO HAVE TO BE PATIENT WITH YOURSELF AND THE OTHERS.

YEAH.

HOW'S SCHOOL GOING?

FINE, I GUESS.

IN ART, MRS. SCOTT GAVE US ALL MIRRORS AND MADE US SIT AND STARE AT OURSELVES FOR FIFTY MINUTES, BECAUSE WE HAVE TO GET TO KNOW OUR FACES BEFORE WE CAN BEGIN OUR SELF-PORTRAITS.

THAT SOUNDS INTENSE.

DID YOU KNOW FACES AREN'T SYMMETRICAL?

I WISH I COULD DRAW SOMEONE ELSE'S FACE. I TRIED TO COUNT MY FRECKLES AND GAVE UP.

YOUR FACE IS MY FAVORITE FACE IN THE WHOLE WORLD.

ARE YOU STILL IN LONDON?

NO, I FLEW TO PARAGUAY YESTERDAY.

I ALREADY PICKED OUT A POSTCARD FOR YOU.

MONKEY MISSES YOU.

I MISS HIM, TOO.

YAWN

LISTEN, WHAT DO YOU THINK ABOUT AUSTRALIA FOR CHRISTMAS?

CAN'T YOU COME HERE THIS YEAR?

IT'LL BE SUMMER IN THE SOUTHERN HEMISPHERE...

SO?

WE CAN HANG OUT WITH SOME ADORABLE WALLABIES.

BUT COOKIE...

YOUR GRANDMA'S GONNA OUTLIVE US ALL.

OKAY, WE DON'T HAVE TO FIGURE THIS OUT RIGHT NOW.

FINE.

I LOVE YOU, KIDDO.

LOVE YOU, TOO.

BOLIVIA

BRAZ

PARAGUAY

...WHEN I'M HOME...

EVERYTHING SEEMS TO BE

RI-IGHT...

WELCOME TO THE HOME OF THE FUTURE.

IN THE UNLIKELY EVENT THAT OUR PLANET SHOULD BECOME TOO TOXIC, WE WILL BLAST OFF INTO SPACE AND DOCK ON THE DARK SIDE OF THE MOON.

HA! THE SOLAR PANELS ARE COOL.

I'LL GIVE YOU THE GRAND TOUR.

FAMILY ROOM.

KITCHEN.

THE HALLWAY. BATHROOM'S THE SECOND DOOR ON THE RIGHT. THAT'S MY ROOM...

...MY BROTHER'S ROOM.

ABANDON ALL HOPE, YE WHO ENTER HERE.

MY PARENTS' ROOM...

AND DOWN THERE'S THE DEN, BUT WE CALL IT THE GUITAR ROOM.

YOUR GUITAR HAS ITS OWN ROOM?

(CHUCKLE) I HAVE MANY GUITARS.

WANNA SEE?

SURE.

MOST OF THEM, WE FIND FOR REALLY CHEAP AND THEN FIX UP.

MY BROTHER'S AN EBAY WIZARD.

!

HOW LONG'VE YOU BEEN COLLECTING THEM?

SINCE I WAS NINE.

THE STRAT, YOU'VE ALREADY MET.

THIS ONE'S MOSTLY FOR SHOW. YOU CAN'T PLAY IT SITTING DOWN.

THE CASINO'S FUN, BUT IT FEEDS BACK WHEN YOU PLAY LOUD.

THIS ONE'S MY GEM: A HAGSTROM VIKING ...

...THE KIND ELVIS PLAYED IN HIS '68 COMEBACK SPECIAL.

IT STILL NEEDS A LITTLE WORK, THOUGH. THE TUNING KNOBS'LL PROBABLY HAVE TO BE REPLACED.

YOU LIKE ELVIS?

IS THAT BAD?

NO... UM...

I LIKE THE STORY OF ELVIS.

SO TRAGIC.

WHAT ABOUT DAVID BOWIE?

JUST IN GENERAL?

ISN'T HE BETTER THAN MARC BOLAN?

BOWIE IS LIKE A SUPERBEING. I'M CONVINCED HE'S FROM ANOTHER PLANET...

...AND THAT'S COOL AND EVERYTHING, BUT FOR ME...

I JUST FEEL MORE REAL LISTENING TO SOMEONE WHO'S HUMAN, WHO'S ALMOST GREAT...

...BUT NOT PERFECT, YOU KNOW?

THAT MAKES SENSE.

IT DOES?

MY MOM LIKES T. REX.

YOU LIVE WITH JUST YOUR DAD, RIGHT?

UH-HUH. MY MOM DOESN'T REALLY LIVE ANYWHERE IN PARTICULAR. SHE TRAVELS. IT'S HER JOB.

I REMEMBER SEEING HER AT SOME SCHOOL THING, LIKE FOREVER AGO.

SHE WAS WEARING THESE AMAZING BOOTS WITH BLACK JEANS AND A LEATHER JACKET.

YEAH, SHE *ALWAYS* WEARS THAT JACKET.

YOU GET TO VISIT HER MUCH?

FOR CHRISTMAS, AND IN THE SUMMER I USUALLY TRAVEL WITH HER FOR A FEW WEEKS.

I'VE NEVER LEFT THE UNITED STATES, AND I'VE ONLY BEEN ON AN AIRPLANE ONCE.

ACCORDING TO MY PARENTS, AIR TRAFFIC LEAVES A HEAVY CARBON FOOTPRINT.

OH.

NO, I MEAN, YOU'RE LUCKY.

I GUESS.

OKAY, TIME TO GET DOWN TO BUSINESS.

ACTUALLY, I HAVEN'T WRITTEN ANY LYRICS YET. I THOUGHT I SHOULD LISTEN TO YOUR SONG AGAIN...

YOU WANT SOME TOTS?

82

YEAH, BUT MAKE EXTRA-EXTRA, BECAUSE I'VE GOT COMPANY.

COMPANY, EH?

DON'T RUN AND HIDE.

CHARLES, THIS IS LUCY...

LUCY... CHARLES...

HOW SWEET, YOU FINALLY MADE A FRIEND.

AND WHAT'S NEW AND EXCITING IN YOUR LIFE?

I THINK I'M IN LOVE WITH FRIDA KAHLO.

scratch scratch

THAT'S GREAT. SHE'S COMPLETELY DEAD AND WILL NEVER LOVE YOU BACK.

I WOULDN'T EXPECT YOU TO UNDERSTAND.

I CAN SMELL YOU FROM HERE. YOU MIGHT WANT TO CHANGE YOUR CLOTHES BEFORE THEY START GROWING MOLD.

WE HAVE ACTUAL WORK TO DO.

CHARLES IS SIMULTANEOUSLY PRETENTIOUS AND IMMATURE— ONE HUNDRED PERCENT OBNOXIOUS.

HE'S BETTER THAN NOTHING.

DON'T EVEN COMPLAIN TO ME ABOUT BEING AN ONLY CHILD.

I'VE BEEN WORKING ON THE SAME RIFF.

WHAT?

I JUST CAN'T GET "YOU ARE MY SUNSHINE" OUT OF MY HEAD.

HA HA HA HA HA HA

KOMM, GIB MIR DEINE HAND.

HUH?!

THAT'S GERMAN FOR "I WANT TO HOLD YOUR HAND."

I HAVEN'T HELD YOUR HAND TO CROSS THE STREET SINCE I WAS, LIKE, THREE!

DON'T!

THE BEATLES WERE ACTUALLY PRESSURED BY THEIR RECORD LABEL TO RELEASE SOME OF THEIR EARLY HITS IN GERMAN.

WIPE

THE ASSUMPTION WAS THAT GERMANS WOULD PREFER IT THAT WAY...

BUT AS IT TURNED OUT, PEOPLE ALL OVER THE WORLD WERE PERFECTLY HAPPY TO LISTEN TO THE BEATLES SING IN ENGLISH.

HI, BEN.

DOORS AND WALLS ARE FOOLS PAPER.

?

HAVE YOU THOUGHT AT ALL ABOUT CHRISTMAS?

NO.

YOUR MOM'S GOING TO CALL TOMORROW, SO YOU MIGHT WANNA THINK ABOUT IT BEFORE THEN.

DON'T YOU WANT THE BREAD?

I HAVE WORK TO DO.

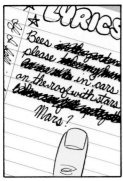

LYRICS

Bees ~~take the gardens~~
please ~~take my hand~~
~~as we walk~~ in cars
on the roof with stars
~~belong to each other~~
Mars?

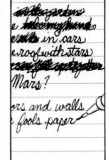

~~take the gardens~~
~~take my hand~~
~~as we walk~~ in cars
~~the~~ roof with stars
~~belong to each other~~
Mars?

~~cars~~ and walls
~~the~~ fools paper

!

HI.

HI.

IT'S A MECHANICAL PENCIL.

Bees in the garden
please bees in my hair
anywhere in car
on the roof with the
clouds go away
Mars?

Doors and wal
are fools paper

RYAN

I'M LUCY.

YOU'RE TWELVE.

YUP. HOW OLD'RE YOU?

FIVE AND A QUARTER.

YOU'RE IN KINDERGARTEN?

UH-HUH.

WHAT'RE YOU DOING?

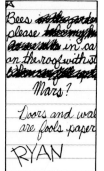
I'M TRYING TO WRITE A SONG.

IT'S NOT GOING SO WELL.

DO YOU WANNA FEED THE DUCKS?

OKAY.

THAT'S MY DAD OVER THERE.

HE HAS THE BREAD IN HIS BAG — YOU JUST HAVE TO ASK HIM FOR IT.

YOU SHOULD ASK HIM.

IF YOU DO IT, I'LL GIVE YOU MY PENCIL.

OKAY.

EXCELLENT JOB!

I JUST FINISHED WORKING ON IT, SO IT'S LIKE A ROUGH DRAFT... I'M NOT SURE...

IT'S GOOD. REALLY GOOD.

IT IS?

I DIDN'T KNOW YOU HAD IT IN YOU. I MEAN, YOU'RE SO NICE.

IT'S NOT A MEAN SONG.

NO, BUT THERE'S PLENTY OF RAGE.

AS LONG AS VANESSA DOESN'T TRY TO SING IT ALL PRETTY...

PLINK PLUNK

LISTEN TO THIS.

BOOM...

BOOM BOOM

NOK NO

TINGA TING TING

BOOM

TINGA

NOK NOK

NOR

MAYBE WE CAN WORK THAT IN SOMEWHERE.

!

CAN I COME IN?...

88

...OR ARE YOU TWO HAVING ANOTHER PRIVATE MEETING?

LOOK, MY DAD SET UP THE PA SYSTEM HE USES AT WORK, SO YOU HAVE A REAL MIC.

TESTING...

RRREEEEE

YOU CAN'T STAND SO CLOSE TO THE SPEAKERS.

WE HAVE LYRICS FOR YOU.

I WOULD JUST CHANGE THIS ONE LINE HERE. INSTEAD OF, "UP WITH THE STARS, WE FLY TO AND FRO," HOW ABOUT, "TIME SEEMS SO SLOW."

YEAH, OKAY.

"DOORS AND WALLS—THEY ARE FOR FOOLS. JUST ASK THE BEES—THEY DON'T FOLLOW RULES."

YOU WROTE THIS?

APPARENTLY, I'M FULL OF RAGE.

HA HA HA!

IF YOU COULD SING IT LIKE HOW YOU DID "MY SUNSHINE"—

YOU KNOW, LIKE, PISSED OFF.

NO PROBLEM, BOSS.

VVRRM

? ?

I'M LATE.

AGAIN.

BUT I HAVE AN AMP.

THAT'LL WORK FOR PRACTICE...

THOUGH IF WE EVER PLAY A GIG...

SEE WHAT I MEAN?

I FOUND THIS ONE ON CRAIGSLIST. MY MOM HAD TO DRIVE ME OUT TO MANTUA TO PICK IT UP.

YOU SHOULD'VE SEEN MY MOM'S FACE WHEN A GUY WITH PINK HAIR AND A NOSE RING OPENED THE DOOR.

THE WHOLE WAY HOME, SHE GAVE ME THIS LECTURE ABOUT THE CHOICES I'M MAKING, AND HOW I NEED TO STAY FOCUSED...

RIGHT. ONLY TWELVE MORE YEARS, AND YOU'LL BE DR. RUPA KHANNA.

OH GOD.

I'VE FIGURED OUT A RIFF THAT I THINK'LL WORK.

OKAY, I CHANGED THE CHORDS JUST A LITTLE...

BECAUSE OF THE "MY SUNSHINE" THING.

RING

OH MY GOD!

I HAVE TO TAKE THIS.

SHE'S BEEN WAITING FOR TREVOR TO CALL ABOUT THE HALLOWEEN DANCE.

ARE YOU GOING?

I GUESS.

I'M *NOT* LOOKING FORWARD TO IT.

YOU'RE GOING?

MY PARENTS ARE MAKING ME.

THEY WANT ME TO TURN OUT BETTER-ADJUSTED THAN MY BROTHER.

KACHANG

ARE YOU DRESSING UP?

I MEAN, IN A COSTUME?

I TOLD MY MOM I'M GOING AS A GHOST...

YOU KNOW, LIKE A WHITE SHEET WITH EYE HOLES.

I'LL PROBABLY WEAR MY GRYFFINDOR SWEATSHIRT.

HE'S COMING!

HE'S BORROWING A BIDDLE CHARTER ID FROM A SEVENTH GRADER WHO HAS A BROKEN LEG OR SOMETHING.

91

YOU GIRLS CAN PAY ME BACK WHEN YOU'RE FAMOUS.

THANKS, MR. KHANNA.

SO HOW'S THE ROCK 'N' ROLL GOING?

WE'RE STILL DEVELOPING OUR SOUND, BUT WE DEFINITELY APPRECIATE CLASSIC ROCK.

OKAY.

I THINK WE'RE GETTING BETTER.

I LIKE THE EAGLES.

ARE YOU GOING TO SOUND LIKE THEM?

I ASK RUPA, AND SHE TELLS ME NOTHING.

REMEMBER WHEN WE USED TO COME HERE...

LIKE, EVERY SINGLE WEEKEND?

YEAH, I GUESS.

WHAT'S WRONG?

NOTHING.

YOU DON'T HAVE TO TRY SO HARD TO BE COOL, YOU KNOW.

YOU WERE FINE HOW YOU WERE BEFORE.

I'M NOT TRYING TO BE COOL, VANESSA.

I'M JUST, I FEEL LIKE, I'M DIFFERENT...

YEAH, I NOTICED.

WELL, GOOD FOR YOU.

I'M GOING TO WALK HOME. ARE YOU COMING?

NO.

DID YOU TELL MOM I WOULD GO TO AUSTRALIA?!

WHAP

NO, I HAVEN'T EVEN ...

I TALKED TO HER, BUNNY. I WANT YOU TO GO. THERE'S NO REASON FOR YOU TO STAY HERE.

WHAT ABOUT WHAT *I* WANT?!

LET'S JUST CALM DOWN FOR A SECOND.

NO!

AND I'M NOT HUNGRY!

SLAM

SHE'S A WOMAN. SHE'S A WOMAN.

BABY'S GOOD TO ME ...

WHOMMP

I'M IN LOVE WITH HER AND I FEEL FINE ...

FLUMP

... I FEEL FINE

SCRRKHHHKH...

KNOCK KNOCK

HI.

HI.

97

SWEETHEART, I'M SORRY. I JUST WANT YOU TO LIVE LIFE TO THE FULLEST. BUT, YOU'RE RIGHT...

CHRISTMAS IS YOUR DECISION.

SOB

WHAT IS IT, BABY?

RUB RUB

NO HALLOWEEN THIS YEAR.

WHAT D'YOU MEAN?

MY SCHOOL'S HAVING A STUPID DANCE INSTEAD.

SNIFF

BOWIE

LIKE A COSTUME PARTY?

A COSTUME *DANCE*.

SNIFF

WELL, WHAT DO YOU WANT TO BE?

NOTHING.

PURRR

!

COME ON, NOW. I ALWAYS MAKE YOUR COSTUME.

purple people eater Halloween 2004

BUT I DON'T DANCE, REMEMBER? THAT'S WHY I PLAY THE DRUMS.

BESIDES, I DON'T WANNA *BE* ANYTHING.

NONSENSE.

PURRR RR RR RR

RINGO!

HUH?

I'LL BE RINGO.

FABULOUS IDEA.

99

LUCY! DINNER'S ALMOST READY!

OKAY, COMING!

WHY DON'T YOU GIVE YOUR MOM A CALL?

I THINK SHE'S IN LONDON FOR A COUPLE NIGHTS.

IT'S ALMOST 11:00 THERE, BUT SHE'S PROBABLY STILL AWAKE.

I DON'T FEEL LIKE IT.

YOU CAN'T KEEP AVOIDING HER.

SHE'S THE ONE ON ANOTHER CONTINENT!

YOUR MOTHER LOVES YOU VERY MUCH.

THAT'S GREAT.

HELLO?

HI, MOM, IT'S ME.

GOD, I MISS YOU. IT'S SO GOOD TO HEAR YOUR VOICE.

I GOT THE PACKAGE.

THANKS FOR ALL THE STUFF.

THAT WOODEN NECKLACE LOOKS LIKE SOMETHING COOKIE WOULD WEAR, HUH?

I'LL GIVE IT TO HER.

SO, THE REINDEER HERDSMEN WERE NICE TO YOU?

THE EVENKI WERE VERY WELCOMING...

BUT IT TURNS OUT REINDEER AREN'T THE FRIENDLIEST OF ANIMALS.

ANYWAY, HOW ARE YOU? HOW'S THE BAND?

FINE. ARE YOU COMING HOME FOR CHRISTMAS?

I DON'T THINK I CAN RESCHEDULE THE AUSTRALIA SHOOT...

JANUARY AND FEBRUARY ARE ALREADY BOOKED...

OKAY.

I'M TRYING... YOU WANNA TALK TO DAD?

TRANS-SIBERIAN

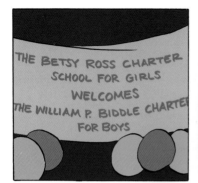

THE BETSY ROSS CHARTER
SCHOOL FOR GIRLS
WELCOMES
THE WILLIAM P. BIDDLE CHARTER
FOR BOYS

HAVE FUN, OKAY?

I'LL BE BACK AT 9:30.

TUG

OKAY.

YOU LOOK GREAT, LUCE. KNOCK 'EM DEAD.

CLICK

BYE, DAD.

LOVE YOU.

!

HEY.

YOU SURVIVING?

SORTA.

MY MOM'S ONE OF THE SPIES.

SHE BROUGHT HER EARPLUGS.

I DON'T BLAME HER.

YOUR MOM'S GONNA BE DISAPPOINTED IF YOU DON'T DANCE WITH THE SURGEON.

HA HA HA HA HA HA HA HA HA HA HA HA HA HA HA HA HA

WHAT A CREEPER!

HEY, LADIES, WANNA PLAY DOCTOR?

GIGGLE

MEANWHILE, VANESSA'S TOTALLY IN HER OWN WORLD.

SO PERFECT. THE CAT AND THE HAT.

HA HA HA HA HA HA HA HA HA

I'M SAYING HELLOOO TO YOU.

...

EVERYBODY LOVES ME, YEAH, CUZ I'M SO FRESH. BETTER THAN A UNICORN IN THE FLESH.

OKAY, SLOW SONG'S OVER — I GUESS IT'S SAFE TO GET UP.

COME ON...

NAH.

GOD...

MISS DEED.

I THOUGHT EVERYONE WAS SUPPOSED TO LIKE MISS DEED.

WHY?!

PRINCESS LEIA... AND...

WHAT'RE YOU?

RINGO.

LET ME GUESS— SHREK?

AND, UH...

A WANNABE BOY WIZARD?

TCH. WHAT'S YOUR PROBLEM?

CHECK THIS OUT.

STINK BOMB

AH, THE BOY WIZARD'S SPECIAL POWER IS THAT HE CAN MAKE THE WORLD SMELL REALLY BAD...

THAT'S ABOUT AS MAGICAL AS, UH...

A SKUNK.

IF YOU'RE GONNA DO THAT, YOU SHOULD WAIT UNTIL SOME NEVER-ENDING SLOW SONG.

LIKE "STAIRWAY TO HEAVEN."

SHE'S RIGHT.

WHEN I GO LIKE THIS, LET HER RIP.

OKAY, PRINCESS.

OUR LOVE IS A PIECE OF GUM RUN OUT OF FLAVOR...

THIS HAS TO BE THE WORST ONE FOR ALL SONG EVER.

UGH, MY BRAIN IS HURTING...

I CAN ACTUALLY FEEL IQ POINTS MELTING AWAY.

NOT YET, HARRY POTTER.

FLIP

IT HASN'T EVEN BEEN AN HOUR YET?!

HOW IS THAT POSSIBLE?

I COULD CALL MY DAD AND HAVE HIM COME EARLY...

NAH, WE CAN DO THIS.

Sigh

YOU KNOW BEN FRANKLIN, THE OLD GUY ON THE BENCH?

YEAH.

HOW OLD D'YOU THINK HE IS?

I DON'T KNOW. OLD-OLD.

WHAT IF HE'S ALWAYS BEEN OLD?

SNOWY WINTER, A PLENTIFUL HARVEST.

THE FIRST SNOWFALL'S SUPPOSED TO COME LATE WEDNESDAY OR EARLY THURSDAY.

NEVER TO LET THE FIRE HAVE PEACE.

THAT DANCE REALLY WORE YOU OUT, HUH?

yawn

IT WAS SO STUPID. I SWEAR, I'M NEVER GOING TO **ANOTHER** ONE.

YOU'RE JUST LIKE YOUR MOTHER.

WHAT D'YOU MEAN?

BECAUSE I WAS THE KID WHO KEPT GOING TO THOSE DANCES, HOPING THE NEXT ONE WOULD BE DIFFERENT.

YOUR MOM SAYS SHE SENT YOU ANOTHER EMAIL.

I KNOW, I KNOW— I'LL WRITE HER BACK. YOU WANT ME TO BCC YOU?

IS IT OKAY IF GEORGIANNA SLEEPS OVER TWO NIGHTS IN A ROW, NOT SCHOOL NIGHTS... ON FRIDAY AND SATURDAY, THE 26TH AND 27TH, I THINK.

THAT'S THANKSGIVING WEEKEND, RIGHT?

YEAH, BUT FRIDAY AND SATURDAY ARE **AFTER** THANKSGIVING.

TECHNICALLY, YES. WHAT ABOUT GEORGIANNA'S FAMILY?

THEY'RE GOING TO A PROTEST FOR SALAMANDERS IN MASSACHUSETTS.

SALAMANDERS?

THERE'S THIS CONSTRUCTION PROJECT THAT'S CUTTING INTO THE HABITAT OF A VERY RARE KIND OF SALAMANDER.

SO CAN SHE STAY WITH US?

I HOPE THESE RARE SALAMANDERS HAVE PURPLE HORNS OR WINGS OR SOMETHING FANTASTIC.

DOES THAT MEAN YES?

ALL RIGHT, ALL RIGHT.

THANKS, DAD.

AREN'T YOU GONNA FEED THE DUCKS?

YEAH, SURE.

CAN I SIT?

THAT LITTLE BOY AND HIS MOTHER WERE HERE EARLIER. YOU JUST MISSED THEM.

!

EIGHT DAYS A WEEK
IS NOT ENOUGH...

$$\begin{array}{r} 1\,1 \\ 3\,6\,5 \\ \times\,1\,2 \\ \hline 7\,3\,0 \\ 3\,6\,5\,0 \\ 4,3\,8\,0 \\ +\;2\,3 \\ \hline 4,4\,0\,3 \end{array}$$

YO!

WHAT?

GEEZ, GOOD TO
SEE YOU, TOO.

I'M TRYING TO FIGURE
SOMETHING OUT.

SOMETHING
IMPORTANT?

I'M 4,403 DAYS
OLD.

HUH, THAT'S A
LOT OF DAYS.

DOES SHE HAVE
TO SIT WITH US
AT LUNCH?

WHAT D'YOU
MEAN?

RUPA FEELS
THE SAME WAY.

WHATEVER.

I'LL TALK TO
HER, I GUESS.

THANKS.

UH-HUH.

I JUST, I CAN'T
BE MYSELF WHEN
SHE'S AROUND.

ARE YOU
SERIOUS?

LUCY!

MOM WANTED ME TO GIVE YOU THIS.

IT'S FROM SIBERIA.

ISN'T THAT SOMETHING.

HOW'S MY GIRL?

FINE.

GREEN TEA?

MY ACUPUNCTURIST MADE THIS BLEND...

TASTES AWFUL, SO IT MUST BE GOOD FOR ME.

AREN'T YOU COLD? WE SHOULD GO INSIDE.

NO, NO...

I'M WAITING FOR THE FIRST SNOW.

BUT THAT'S NOT SUPPOSED TO HAPPEN UNTIL TOMORROW NIGHT.

I CAN FEEL IT COMING.

ANY MINUTE NOW.

COOKIE?

HMM?

YOU'RE MY BEST FRIEND.

WE'RE TWO OLD SOULS, AREN'T WE?

TELL ME THE STORY OF YOUR NAME.

YEARS AGO, WHEN YOU WERE JUST A TINY TOT, I LIKED TO SPOIL YOU BY BRINGING YOU SWEETS.

IT DROVE MOM NUTS, RIGHT?

"YOU'D BE BOUNCING OFF THE WALLS, AND WE'D HAVE TO TAKE YOU TO THE PARK TO LET YOU RUN WILD."

"EVENTUALLY, YOU STARTED ASKING YOUR MOM AND DAD FOR A COOKIE WHEN I WASN'T AROUND."

COOKIE!

"YOUR MOM FINALLY CAVED IN AND BOUGHT SOME ORGANIC BABY BISCUITS."

NO, MAMA. COOKIE!

"WELL, AT FIRST YOUR MOM THOUGHT YOU WERE JUST BEING PICKY—YOU WANTED A **REAL** COOKIE, LIKE THE KIND I BROUGHT TO YOU. BUT..."

NO, I WANT COOKIE!

"AND SO I BECAME COOKIE."

ARE YOU MAD AT MOM?

FOR WHAT?

LEAVING.

Sigh

"OH, SWEETHEART, YOU KNOW I PROBABLY SPENT THE FIRST SIXTEEN YEARS OF YOUR MOTHER'S LIFE BEING MAD AT HER, AND WHAT A WASTE OF TIME THAT WAS. YOUR MOM IS WHO SHE IS AND I LOVE HER FOR IT."

YOU ACTUALLY REMIND ME A LOT OF HER.

WHY?!

"I KNEW IT FROM THE START. AS SOON AS YOUR MOM TOLD ME SHE WAS PREGNANT, I KNEW SHE WAS GOING TO HAVE A GIRL WHO WOULD GIVE HER A REAL RUN FOR HER MONEY."

"AND SURE ENOUGH..."

LUCY!

"OH, HOW YOUR MOM FRETTED OVER YOU."

WHERE'S LUCY?

"HOW YOU MANAGED TO CLIMB IN THAT BIRDBATH REMAINS A MYSTERY."

SHE COULD DROWN!

YOU'RE REALLY THE ONLY PERSON FOR WHOM YOUR MOM HAS EVER CHANGED.

NUH-UH!

"IT'S TRUE—SHE ALWAYS USED TO SAY THAT TAKING PICTURES OF BABIES WAS THE LOWEST FORM OF PHOTOGRAPHY, THEN ALONG CAME YOU."

YOU BETTER WALK HOME, SWEETPEA, BEFORE IT STARTS SNOWING.

IF YOU SAY SO.

?

DAD! LOOK!

122

NOW, SEVENTH GRADERS, REMEMBER TO PAY PARTICULAR ATTENTION TO SELF-PORTRAITS, AND EIGHTH GRADERS, PAY ATTENTION TO REPRESENTATIONS OF WOMEN.

HELLO, LADIES...

ISN'T IT TRUE THAT ALTHOUGH MANET IS CONSIDERED ONE OF THE FIRST IMPRESSIONISTS...

... HE THOUGHT OF HIMSELF AS FIRMLY GROUNDED IN THE CLASSICAL TRADITION OF RENAISSANCE PAINTING?

(SIGH) WELL, YES, THAT *IS* TRUE, BUT HIS PAINTINGS WERE ROUNDLY REJECTED BY THE ART ESTABLISHMENT, AND ARTISTS LIKE MONET AND RENOIR TOUTED HIM AS A MAJOR INFLUENCE.

I THINK I'M ALLERGIC TO MUSEUMS.

ME TOO!

Scratch Scratch

I ALWAYS FEEL LIKE I'M ABOUT READY TO SNEEZE.

IT'S THE LIGHTING OR SOMETHING.

LET'S GET OUT OF HERE FOR A WHILE.

HUH?

COME ON. ERICA'S MOM'S TOO BUSY DROOLING ALL OVER JAKOB TO NOTICE.

MY FRIEND'S A LITTLE DIZZY. SHE NEEDS SOME FRESH AIR—WE'LL BE RIGHT BACK, I PROMISE.

!

?

!

DO YOU SEE WHAT I SEE?

FOUNDER BERNARD BLAKE

UMMM.

IT'S BEN!

OUR BEN, FROM THE PARK!

COME ON, WE'RE FREE!

YOU HUNGRY?

I DIDN'T BRING ANY MONEY.

LUCKY HOTDOG

NO WORRIES, WE CAN SHARE.

A PRETZEL, PLEASE.

Squirt

munch munch

I'M NOT A BIG FAN OF THE IMPRESSIONISTS. ALL THOSE TINY BLOBS.

IT'S LIKE MY DAD'S JAZZ. IF YOU TRY TO FOCUS OR TRY TO HEAR JUST ONE INSTRUMENT, YOU'LL GET A BIG HEADACHE, BUT IF YOU STEP BACK AND JUST LET THE WHOLE THING WASH OVER YOU...

...IT'S ALMOST SOOTHING.

I MISS THE OLD MUSEUM.

Benjamin Franklin Museum

REMEMBER THE MIRRORS AND ALL OF BEN FRANKLIN'S TALENTS FLASHING IN NEON...

AUTHOR, INVENTOR...

FARTER, BEER DRINKER, BELLY SHAKER...

SCIENTIST
CITIZEN
DIPLOMAT
STATESMAN

I USED TO LOVE THAT ROW OF PHONES, WHERE YOU COULD CALL UP DEAD FAMOUS PEOPLE.

DON'T YOU KNOW IT'S NOT SAFE TO GO WANDERING AROUND THE CITY BY YOURSELVES?

HEY, CAMILLE.

WHAT'RE YOU... WHERE'S YOUR PARTNER?

WE DECIDED WE NEEDED SOME TIME APART.

I'M LOOKING FOR A COFFEE SHOP CALLED BLASPHEMOUS RUMOURS.

I TOLD MY FRIEND I'D DROP OFF SOME FLYERS FOR THIS SHOW.

THE SOUND & THE FU
at BLASPHEMOUS RUMO
FRIDAY @ 9pm
with special guests
en Not Include

YOU'RE FRIENDS WITH THE SOUND AND THE FURY?

MY FRIEND CONNOR IS FRIENDS WITH THEIR BASSIST.

WE CAN HELP.

UMMM... I'M GONNA HEAD BACK.

THAT'S SO *INTERESTING*.

EXCUSE ME FOR A MINUTE.

WHAT HAPPENED TO YOU TWO? YOUR FRIEND VANESSA AND I WERE GETTING VERY CONCERNED.

I'M SORRY... I HAVE IRRITABLE BOWEL, AND SOMETIMES...

OH, POOR DEAR.

I'M FEELING BETTER NOW.

THAT WAS GOOD OF YOU TO STAY WITH HER.

YEAH.

DID YOU HEAR THAT VALENTINO ROTH MIGHT BE LEAVING ONE FOR ALL TO START A SOLO CAREER?

NO.

TWO MONTHS AGO YOU WOULD HAVE BEEN DEVASTATED...

BUT NOW THAT YOU'RE SUDDENLY ALL INDIE ROCK, I GUESS YOU'RE TOO COOL FOR SCHOOL...

WHY DON'T YOU MIND YOUR OWN BUSINESS, VANESSA?

YOU'RE THE INTRUDER.

HEY.

WHAT'S UP?

IS THERE ROOM FOR ME HERE?

I GUESS.

YOU SURE YOU WANNA ROCK THE BOAT?

WHATEVER YOU DO, DON'T LOOK OVER AT HER.

WHAT'RE YOU READING?

MY DAD GETS THIS ONE.

REALLY?

UH-HUH.

WASN'T HE ADORABLE?

HE LOOKS LIKE A TEDDY BEAR.

OH MY GOD, YOU'RE RIGHT!

YOU KNOW, THE OLDER I GET, THE MORE I APPRECIATE ELTON JOHN.

EVEN THAT SUPER-CHEESEBALL SONG ABOUT MARILYN MONROE.

!

ONE HUNDRED AND THIRTY-FOUR.

LATER, CHICAS.

SHE'S COUNTING DOWN THE NUMBER OF DAYS LEFT IN THE SCHOOL YEAR.

WOW.

MAYA USED TO BE SUCH A SWEETIE PIE. REMEMBER?

HER FAMILY LOST EVERYTHING IN THE STOCK MARKET CRASH.

THAT'S LIFE.

I GUESS.

CAN WE MAKE SUSHI TOMORROW NIGHT, WHEN GEORGIANNA'S HERE?

I DON'T EVEN WANNA THINK ABOUT ANOTHER MEAL RIGHT NOW.

SHE REALLY, REALLY WANTS TO MEET YOU.

WHO DOES, BUNNY?

GEORGIANNA! SHE PLAYS GUITAR IN MY BAND.

OH, RIGHT.

I CAN'T BELIEVE YOU BROUGHT FOUR PIES!

THAT'S, LIKE, MORE THAN ONE PIE FOR EACH OF US.

I DON'T WANNA THINK ABOUT PIE, EITHER.

ISABEL DIDN'T CALL YET?

SHE CALLED YESTERDAY, FROM THE DESERT.

THE MOJAVE.

I'M ALWAYS A LITTLE RELIEVED WHEN SHE'S BACK IN THE STATES.

WE COULD GIVE *HER* A CALL.

NO, NO.

CAN I HAVE A PIECE OF PUMPKIN PIE?

YOU'RE A BOTTOMLESS PIT!

YOU WANNA PIECE, COOKIE?

GROOAAN

I'VE BEEN MEANING TO TELL YOU TWO... (AHEM)

Sip

I'M NOT GONNA CONTINUE THE CHEMO. MY DOCTOR AND I HAVE DISCUSSED THIS AT LENGTH...

AND IT SEEMS THAT THE CHEMO IS DOING MORE HARM THAN GOOD AT THIS POINT.

IN FACT, THE CANCER HAS A...

ISN'T THERE A DIFFERENT KIND OF CHEMO YOU COULD TRY? YOU CAN'T JUST GIVE UP!

DAD, TELL HER!

LUCY, JUST...

DON'T YOU WANNA GET BETTER?!

LUCY, THAT'S ENOUGH!

WHY'RE YOU ON HER SIDE?!

WE SHOULD CALL ISABEL.

I WILL, I WILL. LATER.

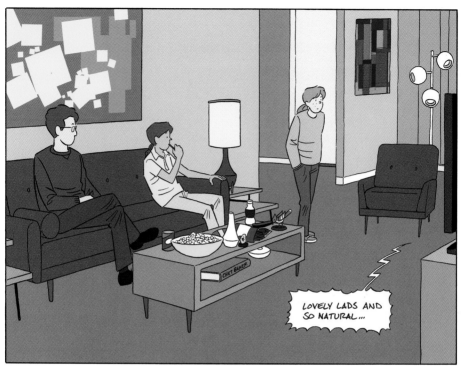

LOVELY LADS AND SO NATURAL...

HMPH!

RED

THANKS.

SHE HAD MY FINGER, YOU KNOW...

CAN WE WATCH IT AGAIN?

ARE YOU SURE YOU DON'T WANNA EAT SOME REAL FOOD OR, LIKE, STEP OUTSIDE?

IT'S ALL WARM AND SUNNY AGAIN.

NAH.

OKAY, GIRLS, I HAVE A BIT OF WORK TO DO. IF YOU NEED ME, I'LL BE UPSTAIRS IN MY OFFICE.

YOUR DAD'S REALLY NICE.

YEAH, YEAH, I KNOW.

WE HAD A GOOD CHAT ABOUT PHIL SPECTOR.

WHO?

"ECCENTRIC GENIUS MUSIC PRODUCER IN THE FIFTIES, SIXTIES, AND SEVENTIES. HE CREATED THE **WALL OF SOUND**, WHICH INFLUENCED EVERYONE. I MEAN **EVERYONE.**"

"FROM THE BEACH BOYS TO THE JESUS AND MARY CHAIN."

"EVENTUALLY, IN TYPICALLY WEIRD HOLLYWOOD FASHION, HE WAS CONVICTED OF MURDERING AN ACTRESS IN HIS LA MANSION."

SPECTOR P.
LOS ANGELES PD
3421569

WHY DIDN'T YOU TELL ME YOUR GRANDMA'S SICK?

I THOUGHT SHE WAS GETTING BETTER.

WHEN CAN I MEET HER?

I DUNNO.

LUTZ

HALT!

HALT?!

WHAT HAS SHE DONE WITH THE RING?!

HELP!

I THINK THIS IS MY ABSOLUTE FAVORITE PART.

HERE I STAND HEAD IN HAND...

♩ ♩ ♩

WAIT!

Klik

THE FLUTE GUY... DOESN'T HE LOOK LIKE A YOUNGER VERSION OF BEN FRANKLIN?

I THOUGHT YOU DECIDED HE WAS NEVER YOUNG. YOU'RE LOSING IT, MY FRIEND!

OH, GUESS WHAT? MY BROTHER'S IN LOVE WITH A POSSIBLY REAL PERSON.

WITH WHO? HOW?

LAZYJANE93—HE FOUND HER ONLINE, OF COURSE.

SHE'S SUPPOSEDLY A NINETEEN-YEAR-OLD CHICK IN PROVIDENCE, BUT FOR ALL WE KNOW, SHE'S A MIDDLE-AGED DUDE IN TOPEKA.

GIGGLE GIGGLE

I MEAN, SHE'S TOO PERFECT. WHAT REAL GIRL KNOWS WEEN'S WHOLE CATALOGUE?

YOU?!

GIGGLE GIGGLE

HA HA HA HA HA HA HA HA HA

137

OKAY, IF YOU TWO ARE GONNA TELL SECRETS, THEN I'M GONNA READ MY BOOK AND IGNORE YOU.

OH, THAT'S A PAGE-TURNER.

YOU READ THIS?

WHEN IT FIRST CAME OUT.

LOVE GOES TO BUILDINGS ON FIRE

FIVE YEARS IN NEW YORK THAT...

HELLO!

OH, EMILY, HI!

Giggle

nudge

138

CAN YOU BELIEVE THIS WEATHER?

I MUST ADMIT I'M ENJOYING IT... THOUGH IT'S KIND OF EERIE.

SHOULDN'T THEY'VE MIGRATED BY NOW?

I KNOW. I FEEL LIKE I'M IN A HITCHCOCK MOVIE.

HA HA!

LET'S GO FEED THE DUCKS!

I FORGOT TO INTRODUCE YOU. RYAN, THIS IS MY FRIEND GEORGIANNA.

HI, RYAN. I PROMISE I DON'T BITE. WELL, SOMETIMES I BITE THE BAD GUYS, BUT USUALLY I CAN'T CATCH THEM. THEY'RE ALWAYS GETTING AWAY.

HOW OLD'RE YOU?

FORTY-THREE.

NUH-UH.

UH-HUH.

139

I'VE JUST ABOUT MASTERED RINGO'S DRUMBEAT FROM "TICKET TO RIDE."

THAT'S A GOOD ONE...

ACTUALLY REALLY INNOVATIVE FOR ITS TIME.

RYAN, HONEY, WE HAVE TO GET GOING. THAT BIRTHDAY PARTY STARTS IN LESS THAN AN HOUR AND WE STILL HAVE TO FIGURE OUT A PRESENT.

BUT I DON'T EVEN LIKE SASHA!

THAT ISN'T TRUE.

COME ON NOW, WE RSVP'D.

BYE, GIRLS! HAVE A GOOD AFTERNOON.

BYE!

Whisper Whisper

DID YOU GET HER NUMBER?

PLEASE TELL ME YOU AT LEAST GOT HER EMAIL.

WELL, TELL US ABOUT HER! WHERE'S SHE FROM? WHAT DOES SHE DO?

I'VE HARDLY SPOKEN TO HER!

SHE WORKS AS A FILM ARCHIVIST AT PENN.

THAT'S COOL! RIGHT?

140

WE'RE GONNA GO SHOPPING, OKAY?

SHOPPING?

JUST AROUND THE SQUARE. WE'LL MEET YOU BACK AT THE HOUSE.

OH, OKAY.

GET WHAT YOU CAN, AND WHAT YOU GET, HOLD.

REALLY?

DON'T BE SQUEAMISH.

STORE A
DONATIO

BUT WE DON'T EVEN KNOW IF THIS STUFF FITS.

DOESN'T MATTER.

DING DONG

I'M SORRY...

I RUINED THANKSGIVING.

I'M THE ONE WHO FREAKED OUT.

YOU MUST BE... CAROLINA?

GEORGIANNA.

CALL ME COOKIE.

NICE TO MEET YOU.

LIKEWISE, DEAR.

WHY DOES IT SMELL SO DELICIOUS IN HERE?

HAVE YOU BEEN...

WHOA!

!

THE PAST COUPLE OF DAYS I'VE BEEN IN A BIT OF A BAKING FRENZY.

ARE YOU GIRLS HUNGRY?

SNICKERDOODLES, LEMON POPPY SEED, CHOCOLATE CHIP, DOUBLE CHOCOLATE CHIP, CHOCOLATE LAVA, PEANUT BUTTER CRUNCH, M&M, AND THOSE ARE SOME KIND OF HAZELNUT EXPERIMENT.

I'LL POUR YOU A GLASS OF MILK.

MY APPETITE SEEMS TO BE IMPROVING.

THIS IS THE BEST THING I'VE EVER TASTED IN MY LIFE!

I'M GLAD TO HEAR IT!

WANNA SEE OUR NEW CLOTHES?

LET ME AT LEAST HEM THOSE FOR YOU, SWEETHEART.

CAN YOU TEACH ME HOW TO SEW?

ME, TOO!

WHAT A SHAME THEY DON'T TEACH HANDCRAFTS IN SCHOOL ANYMORE. AND MY WORD, AT YOUR SCHOOL, ESPECIALLY—BETSY ROSS, THE PATRIOTIC SEAMSTRESS...

... AND NONE OF YOU KIDS KNOW YOUR WAY AROUND A BOBBIN.

I'M NOT GOING TO ANSWER THAT WHILE I HAVE COMPANY.

RING RING

IT'S OKAY, COOKIE...

CLICK

MOM, IT'S ME AGAIN. I KNOW YOU'RE THERE... ALL RIGHT, THEN CALL ME BACK OR DON'T CALL ME BACK. I GUESS YOU WIN, BECAUSE I'M DONE PLAYING THIS GAME...

WHAT'S GOING ON?

OH, YOUR MOTHER... I'LL NEVER UNDERSTAND HER.

ARE YOU GOING TO CALL HER BACK?

I WILL—LATER.

YOU OKAY, KIDDO?

I WISH GEORGIANNA WERE STILL HERE.

YOU'LL SEE HER AT SCHOOL TOMORROW.

IS COOKIE GOING TO BE OKAY?

I DON'T KNOW.

GOD, I HOPE SO.

WILL YOU GET ME A GLASS OF WATER? PLEASE?

SURE THING.

I CAN'T SLEEP. MY BRAIN WON'T TURN OFF.

I KNOW WHAT YOU MEAN.

JULIE ANDREWS

DAD?

YEAH?

WHAT'S YOUR FAVORITE BEATLES SONG?

OH, GOOD, ANOTHER QUESTION I CAN'T ANSWER.

WHY NOT?

BECAUSE MY FAVORITE SONG PROBABLY CHANGES EVERY DAY, EVERY MINUTE, ALL DEPENDING ON MY MOOD.

WELL, WHAT'S YOUR FAVORITE SONG RIGHT NOW, THIS VERY SECOND?

HANG ON...

YAWN

I ONCE HAD A GIRL...

THIS SONG MAKES ME FEEL LIKE WALKING AROUND BAREFOOT AND GROWING A BEARD.

YOU ALREADY HAVE A BEARD, MR. FUZZHEAD.

MRROW

THAT'S A SITAR, RIGHT?

DOES THIS RING MEAN ANYTHING TO YOU?

UH HUH.

PAT PAT

HI.

OH, HEY. YOU HAVE
A GOOD THANKSGIVING?

I GUESS SO. MY DAD
AND I BEAT MY MOM
AND BROTHER AT
TRIVIAL PURSUIT, AS
USUAL.

NICE.

ARE THOSE PANTS FROM
YOUR HALLOWEEN COSTUME?

UH-HUH.

SORRY TO HEAR
ABOUT COOKIE.

WHAT D'YOU
MEAN?

GEORGIANNA TOLD ME THIS MORNING IN MATH.

SLAM

I LOVE COOKIE, TOO, YOU KNOW.

WHY'RE YOU TALKING ABOUT HER LIKE THAT?! SHE'S GOING TO BE FINE!

REMEMBER THAT ONE TIME SHE HAD US OVER TO MAKE GINGERBREAD HOUSES...

AND WE ATE ABOUT HALF THE CANDY AND FROSTING, AND I GOT THE WORST STOMACH ACHE...

WHY'S EVERYTHING ALWAYS ABOUT YOU?!

IT'S NOT!

RRRRIIIIINNNNNGGG

EVERYONE'S TALKING ABOUT HOW YOU'RE GEORGIANNA'S LITTLE PET. YOU FOLLOW HER AROUND LIKE A PUPPY ON A LEASH.

YOU'RE JUST JEALOUS.

HA HA!

SEE YA.

QUICKAROO

LUCY!

YOU'RE OKAY?

UH-HUH.

YOU'RE FREEZING! WHAT HAPPENED?

NOTHING...

I WAS JUST WALKING AROUND...

I NEEDED TO WALK.

THE SCHOOL CALLED ME AT WORK, AND I DROVE HOME RIGHT AWAY.

I'VE JUST BEEN...

GOD, I'VE BEEN...

LUCY, THIS IS SERIOUS!

I CALLED EVERYONE!

I CALLED THE POLICE!

WHERE'S YOUR PHONE?

I...

WHERE'S YOUR COAT?

IN MY LOCKER. I HAD TO LEAVE. I NEEDED SOME AIR. I'M SORRY.

SOME AIR?!

I'M SORRY!

I DON'T UNDERSTAND WHAT HAPPENED!

I TOLD YOU!

I WAS SO WORRIED.

ALL SALES FINAL

Z

YOU MUST LET ME SLEEP NOW FOR THE WINTER.

WHERE YOU GOING?

TO MY NEST.

winter

YOU SLEPT FOR NEARLY EIGHTEEN HOURS.

YAWN
THEN WHY'M I STILL TIRED?
YOU HUNGRY?
DON'T YOU HAVE TO GET TO WORK?
NO, I'M IN THE MIDDLE OF A FAMILY CRISIS.

CRISIS?

LISTEN, I JUST TALKED TO THE SCHOOL. THEY WERE VERY UNDER-STANDING, GIVEN THE CIRCUMSTANCES.

IF YOU'RE FEELING OKAY, YOU CAN GO BACK TOMORROW.
YOU DON'T FEEL WARM.
I'M NOT SICK.

HOW ABOUT SOME EGGS?

PANCAKES?

ALL RIGHT.

RING

IT'S COOKIE. WANT ME TO ANSWER?
RING

NO, I BETTER TAKE IT.

WHY?

I'M SORRY YOU'RE...

I'M NOT UPSET, DANIEL!

I DIDN'T GET THE IMPRESSION THAT ISABEL WAS FREAKING OUT WHEN I—

...

I THOUGHT SHE DESERVED TO KNOW WHAT'S—

NO, I HAVEN'T TALKED TO LUCY YET—

...

FINE THEN, ELEANOR, IF YOU SAY SO.

BEEP

WHAT DID YOU DO?!

WHAT DID I DO?! HA!

YOUR GRANDMA HAS BEEN AVOIDING YOUR MOM, SO YOUR MOM CALLED ME, AND AFTER WE TALKED, YOUR MOM DECIDED, OF HER OWN ACCORD, TO COME HOME FOR CHRISTMAS.

JUST BECAUSE I WALKED AWAY FROM SCHOOL?

NO, LUCY, BECAUSE OF COOKIE'S CANCER.

MOM THINKS COOKIE'S
GOING TO DIE!

TO MY
NEST.

!

Flump

WHAT ON EARTH
ARE YOU DOING?!

I'M JUST GONNA WALK
TO THE PARK.
I'LL BE RIGHT BACK,
I PROMISE.

YOU'RE NOT GOING
ANYWHERE!

AM I GROUNDED?

FOR THE NEXT TWO WEEKS,
I WANT YOU TO COME STRAIGHT
HOME AFTER SCHOOL. NO
HANGING OUT WITH FRIENDS.
YOU CAN STILL HAVE BAND
PRACTICE, BUT THAT'S IT.

COME EAT THESE PANCAKES!

I THOUGHT YOU WANTED YOUR MOM HOME FOR CHRISTMAS.

NOT ANYMORE.

Chomp Chomp

Slap

3:52

IT'S RUPA.

THANKS.

FIVE MINUTES!

HEY.

HOW *ARE* YOU?

BETTER, I GUESS. I JUST NEEDED SOME TIME ALONE.

I WAS, BUT I'M NOT ANYMORE.

ARE YOU COMING BACK TOMORROW?

PROBABLY.

I GOTTA GO. I'M SUPPOSED TO BE TAKING AN SSAT PRACTICE TEST.

OKAY, BYE.

RINNNG

IT'S GEORGIANNA.

TWO MINUTES!

HI.

I'M SORRY I TOLD VANESSA ABOUT COOKIE. I JUST THOUGHT...

IT'S OKAY. I CAN ONLY TALK FOR A MINUTE, AND I NEED YOU TO DO ME A FAVOR.

WHAT?

WILL YOU RUN DOWN TO THE PARK AND SEE IF BEN'S ON HIS BENCH? I HAD THIS DREAM...

IT'S TWO DEGREES OUTSIDE!

UGH, FINE. BUT YOU'RE CRAZY.

CALL ME BACK.

5:58

RINNG

SO?

DON'T PANIC, BUT HE'S NOT THERE.

167

YOU'RE REALLY STRUGGLING WITH THIS.

CAN I DRAW SOMEONE ELSE? LIKE MY MOM, OR MY GRANDMA...

OR ANYONE? PLEASE?

HOW ABOUT IF YOU BEGIN BY DRAWING YOUR MOM OR YOUR GRANDMA AND SEE IF THAT HELPS YOU TO DRAW YOURSELF?

DRAWING IS A PROCESS. YOU HAVE TO LET YOURSELF TRUST THE PROCESS.

I CAN'T.

NO, YOU DON'T WANT TO, WHICH IS VERY DIFFERENT.

I NEED A BOOK ABOUT SURREAL ART.

SURE.

FOLLOW ME THIS WAY.

?

FRIDA KHALO

I'M PROBABLY GONNA FAIL ART.

I DON'T THINK THAT'S POSSIBLE.

 ANYTHING'S POSSIBLE IF YOU PUT YOUR MIND TO IT.

 I *NEED* A PIECE OF GUM.

!

 IS THAT SO?

 I HAVE A.D.D., AND CHEWING HELPS ME CONCENTRATE.

 OH, I'VE BEEN MEANING TO TELL YOU—I ALWAYS THOUGHT THE TIME SERIES WAS A TRILOGY, BUT IT TURNS OUT THERE ARE TWO MORE BOOKS AFTER *A SWIFTLY TILTING PLANET*, WHICH MAKES IT, WHAT, A QUINTET, I GUESS.

 RIGHT. *MANY WATERS* AND *AN ACCEPTABLE TIME.*

YOU'VE READ THEM?

 NOT YET. WHY NOT?

 BECAUSE I'M SAVING THEM... FOR LATER.

 YOU'RE A REAL ENIGMA, LUCY SUTCLIFFE.

BEEP

 I KNOW. CAN I PLEASE HAVE A PIECE OF GUM?

enigma /ɪˈnɪgmə/ *nou*

1. an obscure spee writing 2. somethi to understand or 3. an inscrutable person (*to his frie* always something **synonyms**: conu puzzle, riddle, se from Latin *aenig* ainigmat- ainigm to speak in ridd **first known use**

YOU DO KNOW MR. DOYLE IS GAY.

YEAH?

SO WHY'RE YOU FLIRTING WITH HIM?

I WASN'T.

RIIIIIIIIIINNNG

BETSY ROSS
SCHOOL FOR GIRLS K-8

I'VE JUST SEEN A FACE...

LUCY!

170

AND I COULD ANSWER BEFORE HE DOES. THEN HE'D KNOW THAT I KNOW.

giggle giggle giggle snort giggle

ALL SALES FINAL

EXCUSE ME.

WHAT BAND IS THIS?

?!

INTERPOL.

I LIKE THIS SONG.

YEAH.

STELLA, STELLA-AH!

WILL YOU TELL YOUR BROTHER I HAVE AN EXTRA TICKET FOR THE SOUND AND THE FURY ON FRIDAY?

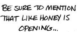

BE SURE TO MENTION THAT LIKE HONEY IS OPENING...

AND THAT IF YOU CLOSE YOUR EYES YOU CAN BASICALLY PRETEND YOU'RE AT A JESUS AND MARY CHAIN CONCERT...

OKAY.

ALL SALES FINAL

!

WE GOTTA GO?!

giggle giggle giggle

I WAS JUST MESSING AROUND.

WE'RE HAVING PRACTICE, RIGHT? RUPA SAID—

YEAH.

IS IT NOON ALREADY?

ALMOST.

SO WHAT'S UP?

I WROTE SOME MORE LYRICS.

I MEANT, LIKE, IN GENERAL— HOW'S LIFE?

MY MOM'S COMING HOME FOR CHRISTMAS.

SHE IS? WHEN? NEXT WEEK.

BUT I'M GOING TO BE AT SNO MOUNTAIN.

OH, WELL.

WHY'RE YOU BEING LIKE THIS?

LIKE WHAT?

Song two

I dreamt I brought you a cup of tea.
You drank it all and then you gave your ring to me.
yeah, your ring to me.
I watched you climb the

176

VANESSA, THIS IS MY BROTHER, CHARLES. CHARLES, VANESSA.

HEY.

DID YOU JUST ROLL OUT OF BED?

NO, I'VE BEEN UP FOREVER, I—

SO, AN HOUR AND A HALF? YEAH.

NEW LYRICS?

I WROTE THEM THIS MORNING.

WHO'S THIS ABOUT?

I HAD THIS DREAM—

I THINK MY BROTHER LIKES YOU.

I KNOW WHO...

WE FOUND A REAL-LIFE MUSE. HE WORKS AT...

IT'S NOT ABOUT CONNOR.

CONNOR?

Song two

dreamt I brought you
a cup of tea.
drank it all and th
you gave your ring,
yeah, your ring to me
watched you climb t
tallest tree.
higher and higher in
the night.
his fire burns like

LUCY AND CONNOR SITTING IN A TREE!

K-I-S-S-I-N-G.

"THIS FIRE BURNS LIKE A TIGER."

WILLIAM BLAKE, REMEMBER?

"TYGER, TYGER, BURNING BRIGHT."

MRS. CLARKE WOULD BE SO PROUD.

SHUT UP!

NO, I LIKE IT!

ME, TOO.

YOU DO?

YEAH.

VRRM

I THINK THE BUNNY SLIPPERS SHOULD BE A THING.

!

LIKE, YOU SHOULD WEAR THEM IF WE EVER PLAY OUTSIDE THIS GARAGE.

UM, NO.

JUST ONCE, I WANT TO BE THE FIRST TO ARRIVE. WHAT'D I MISS?

WE HAVE A NEW SONG...

AND LUCY'S IN LOVE WITH SOMEBODY NAMED CONNOR.

THANKS A LOT.

YOU LOOK FANCY.

I HAD MY INFORMATIONAL INTERVIEW AT PARK ACADEMY THIS MORNING.

OH, YEAH. HOW'D IT GO?

RIIING

I'LL BE RIGHT BACK.

TREVOR'S BEEN TRYING REALLY HARD TO PROVE HE'S NOT A JERK.

WHY IS SHE EVEN TALKING TO HIM?

UNLESS SHE HAS A SECRET PLAN TO ACT ALL LOVEY AND THEN SUDDENLY CRUSH HIM.

I DOUBT IT.

I DIDN'T KNOW PARK INTERVIEWED SEVENTH GRADERS.

THEY MADE AN EXCEPTION...

I TOLD HIM I'M BUSY.

YEAH, FOR THE REST OF YOUR LIFE!

DOESN'T CONNOR GO TO ALL SAINTS?

OH MY GOD, LUCY, YOU'RE BRILLIANT!

I GUESS NOW YOU WANT ME TO HANG OUT WITH TREVOR?

ARE WE GONNA PRACTICE OR WHAT?

... SO VANESSA HAD THIS IDEA THAT THE BAND COULD PLAY FOR YOUR MOM WHILE SHE'S IN TOWN AND...

WHY?

I DON'T KNOW.

IT WOULD BE GOOD PRACTICE, AND I WAS THINKING MAYBE WE COULD HAVE A MINI-SHOW FOR OUR FAMILIES.

COOKIE COULD COME, AND MY BROTHER, AND MY PARENTS, IF THEY'RE AROUND, AND MAYBE WE COULD WIN OVER RUPA'S MOM...

I HEARD RUPA'S SKIPPING EIGHTH GRADE AND STARTING PARK ACADEMY NEXT YEAR.

WHO TOLD YOU THAT?

I HEARD HER TALKING TO VANESSA.

WELL, SHE MUST'VE BEEN JOKING. SOMETIMES IT'S HARD TO TELL WITH HER.

LUCY, SHE HAD THE INTERVIEW.

BUT SHE WOULD'VE SAID SOMETHING TO ME.

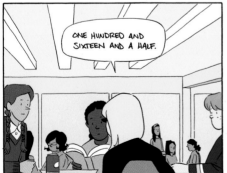

ONE HUNDRED AND SIXTEEN AND A HALF.

PEACE, CHICAS.

ANY BIG NEWS? LIKE WHAT?

ARE YOU STARTING PARK NEXT YEAR? PROBABLY.

YOU WANT TO SKIP EIGHTH GRADE?

YEAH, I CAN'T WAIT TO BE THE YOUNGEST *AND* MOST AWKWARD GIRL IN HIGH SCHOOL.

(SIGH) AS IF WHAT I WANT MATTERS...

IT DOES! NO, IT REALLY DOESN'T.

YOU KNEW ABOUT THIS?! I KNEW IT WAS A POSSIBILITY.

WHY DIDN'T YOU *TELL* ME?! LIKE YOU'RE SO COMMUNICATIVE.

WELL, WE CAN'T LET HER DO IT.

OH, BY THE WAY, TREVOR KNOWS CONNOR. BUT NOT VERY WELL. I MEAN, THEY'RE NOT FRIENDS.

ANYWAY, IF RUPA HAS DECIDED TO LEAVE, HOW COULD WE STOP HER?

YOU NEVER DRINK WINE.

I DO, TOO.

THAT'S THE KIND MOM LIKES.

I LIKE IT, TOO!

SPAGHETTI IS MOM'S FAVORITE.

AND YOURS.

HMPH.

WHY'RE YOU SO DETERMINED TO HAVE A LOUSY TIME TONIGHT?

WILL YOU PLEASE LET THEM IN?

LUCY!

HI, MOM.

YOU'RE SO TALL.

I'M BASICALLY THE SHORTEST PERSON IN MY CLASS, SO...

HELLO, HELLO.

I'VE MISSED YOU TOO, BUDDY.

I BROUGHT TIRAMISU!

OF COURSE, YOU DID!

LET ME TAKE YOUR COATS.

COOL.

THANKS.

I CAN'T BELIEVE THE FIRST VINYL COPIES OF THIS ALBUM ACTUALLY HAD A PEELABLE BANANA.

SPEAKING OF VINYL, ALL OUR OLD RECORDS ARE STILL UP IN THE LINEN CLOSET.

WE SHOULD GO THROUGH THOSE...

THERE ARE SOME REAL GEMS.

Y'KNOW THAT MOE TUCKER PLAYED HER DRUMS STANDING UP?

TELL US ABOUT YOUR TRAVELS.

I FEEL LIKE I SPEND MORE TIME IN AIRPORTS THAN ANYWHERE ELSE...

HAVE YOU HEARD ABOUT HER SIDE PROJECT?

OH, MOM.

IT'S NOTHING.

DING

TELL US!

I'VE BEEN TAKING PHOTOS OF PEOPLE SLEEPING IN AIRPORTS...

I HAVEN'T WORKED ON A SOLO PROJECT IN FOREVER, SO I......

WHAT BAND IS THIS?

INTERPOL.

I LIKE THIS SONG. THE GUITARS AND BASS SOUND SO DENSE TOGETHER.

I KNOW, RIGHT? A WALL OF SOUND.

JUST WHAT I WAS THINKING, BUT LESS PHIL SPECTOR AND MORE JESUS AND MARY CHAIN.

YEAH, "PSYCHOCANDY." HAVE YOU HEARD THE BAND LIKE HONEY?

NO.

THEY'RE LOCAL. THEY'RE PLAYING DOWNTOWN NEXT THURSDAY AT THE ROMPER ROOM. IT'S ALL AGES IF YOU WANNA GO.

Flip

YEAH, FOR SURE!

WHAT DO YOU THINK, LUCE?

HUH?

"THE NUTCRACKER..." FOR OLD TIME'S SAKE. MAYBE VANESSA WOULD LIKE TO COME, TOO?

SHE'S GOING SKIING WITH HER FAMILY.

THEN JUST THE TWO OF US?

IF YOU WANT TO...

I WENT TO SEE IT IN LONDON EARLIER THIS MONTH, BUT THE STAGING WAS MODERN AND MINIMALIST...

IT JUST DIDN'T SEEM QUITE RIGHT.

YOU'VE BEEN SPENDING A LOT OF TIME IN LONDON.

I GUESS SO.

ARE YOU STILL DATING THAT ONE GUY?

IT'S NOTHING SERIOUS.

I'M REALLY FULL. CAN I BE EXCUSED?

LUCY...

THAT'S OKAY. GO AHEAD, KIDDO.

DID I TELL YOU WHO I SAW ON MY FLIGHT TO BERLIN?

YOU SAY YOU'VE SEEN SEVEN WONDERS... ♪

BUT YOU CAN'T SEE ME!

NO WAY, THERE'S A SONG CALLED "MY DING-A-LING."

WHAT?!

YUP—IT'S EXACTLY WHAT YOU'RE THINKING.

WHERE'S "PURPLE PEOPLE EATER?" WHO DOES THAT ONE?

SHEB WOOLEY.

HERE.

WE HAVE ONE MORE. YOU PICK!

HOW ABOUT "PRETTY LITTLE ANGEL EYES"? UH, CURTIS LEE, I THINK.

YOU LADIES READY TO ORDER?

TO KNOW, KNOW, KNOW HIM IS TO LOVE, LOVE, LOVE HIM...

I'LL HAVE A TURKEY BURGER, MEDIUM-WELL, AND A SIDE OF COLESLAW.

A VEGGIE BURGER, PLEASE, WITH CURLY FRIES.

GRILLED CHEESE AND A SIDE OF FRUIT.

FRUIT?

MARASCHINO CHERRIES AND PINEAPPLE!

CAN WE ALSO GET THE BLOOMING ONION?

ALL RIGHT. WE'LL START WITH THAT *THING*.

SOUNDS GOOD.

I CAN'T BELIEVE YOU HAVE THREE CHRISTMAS TREES...

TWO.

COOKIE'S COUNTS AS THREE.

NO, IT DOESN'T, AND THE TREE IN MY ROOM IS TINY.

MY PARENTS THINK IT'S WRONG TO *SLAUGHTER* TREES— THEY RUIN ANYTHING FUN.

IF OUR PARENTS WERE PERFECT, THEN WE WOULDN'T BE VERY INTERESTING PEOPLE, WOULD WE?

I COULD HANDLE BEING A LITTLE LESS INTERESTING. LUCY TOLD ME YOU LIKE T. REX?

YEAH! GOD, I HAVEN'T LISTENED TO THEM IN FOREVER...

WE STILL HAVE TO GO THROUGH MY OLD RECORDS.

"BACK IN THE 80s, ALL THE COOL KIDS WERE LISTENING TO R.E.M. AND THE SMITHS AND THE PIXIES. I WAS LISTENING TO T. REX."

THIS ONE TIME IN COLLEGE, I THOUGHT I SAW MARC BOLAN'S GHOST.

WHERE?

"NEW YORK—THE BOWERY. HE HAD THE HAIR, BUT KIND OF SALT AND PEPPERY, AND HE WAS WEARING THIS JEAN JACKET THAT WAS TOO SMALL FOR HIM. I FOLLOWED HIM FOR BLOCKS UNTIL I WAS LOST, AND THEN WHEN I STOPPED, HE TURNED AROUND AND WAVED AT ME..."

MAYBE IT WAS REALLY HIM... LIKE HE FAKED HIS DEATH SO HE COULD SECRETLY CONTINUE MAKING MUSIC IN PEACEFUL OBSCURITY.

I LIKE THE WAY YOU THINK.

"SO, ANYWAY, I DUCKED INTO A DIVE BAR TO GET MY BEARINGS..."

AND THAT'S WHERE I ENDED UP MEETING YOUR FATHER. NOT THAT NIGHT, BUT LATER THAT SAME SUMMER.

WE STILL HAVEN'T GOTTEN YOUR MOM ANYTHING FOR CHRISTMAS.

HMMM.

I'M SERIOUS. ANY IDEAS?

SOME FANCY LOTION OR SOAP OR SOMETHING?

IS IT OKAY IF I GO ON A QUICK WALK? I'LL BUNDLE UP.

CAN I COME?

I JUST NEED TO GET SOME AIR... BY MYSELF.

ALL RIGHT.

PAST MAS
PLEASE PL
► REVOLVER
RUBBER S
SGT PEPP
WITH THE

MENU

I WAS ALONE.
I TOOK A RIDE.

und of
Music

DO YOU EVER FEEL LIKE YOU HAVE ABSOLUTELY NOTHING TO SAY... TO ANYONE?

DID THE WALK HELP?

I JUST WANNA BE EXCITING...

YOU ARE!

NO, I'M NOT. I OVERTHINK EVERYTHING, AND THEN I'M JUST BORING.

SIGH

THAT'S KINDA COOL.

LIGHTHEARTED BUT NOT TOO JOKEY, RIGHT?

SURE.

COOKIE'S NOT GETTING BETTER, SO DOES THAT MEAN SHE'S DYING?

YOU DON'T HAVE TO SAY IT. I KNOW.

I NEED A HOT COCOA REFILL.

I'LL GET IT. ANYBODY ELSE WANT ANYTHING?

EGG NOG? TEA? WINE?

... MAY I INTRODUCE TO YOU ...

I'LL HAVE A LITTLE MORE EGGNOG.

DO WE HAVE ANY BACARDI?

PROBABLY.

SGT. PEPPER'S LONELY HEARTS CLUB BAND

195

THANK YOU, MY LOVELIES.

YOU'RE WELCOME.

Y'GET IT— TUBE SOCKS?

VERY NICE.

I GUESS I WENT A LITTLE CRAZY AT THE TRANSPORTATION MUSEUM.

WHY DON'T YOU OPEN THAT BIG ONE?

OKAY!

YOU MADE THIS?!

YOUR MOM HELPED.

SHE STAYED UP ALL NIGHT FINISHING IT.

TRY IT ON— LET'S SEE!

THIS IS THE BEST PRESENT EVER!

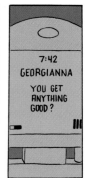
7:42
GEORGIANNA
YOU GET ANYTHING GOOD?

IT'S STRANGE TO BE MIDDLE-AGED, ISN'T IT?

KIND OF.

I JUST FEEL SO MUCH CALMER.

YEAH, Y'KNOW, I'M ACTUALLY LOOKING FORWARD TO BECOMING A WEIRD, OLD LADY.

7:45
GEORGIANNA
MY PARENTS ARE THE MOST PRACTICAL GIFT GIVERS.

Klik

Klik

Klik

Klik

Klik

Z Z Z Z Z

SNAP

I THINK THAT'S RUDE!

COOKIE WON'T MIND...

I'M DEFINITELY NOT SPENDING THE NIGHT HERE. I DON'T WANT ANYONE TAKING PICTURES OF **ME** WHEN I'M ASLEEP.

LUCY, DON'T BE...

I'M NOT BEING **DRAMATIC!**

?

DAD?

DAD?!

I'M UP HERE!

ARE YOU SICK?

SIGH

YOU'RE DEPRESSED BECAUSE MOM LEFT.

I'M JUST FEELING A LITTLE... WORN OUT.

THE HOLIDAYS ALWAYS DO THIS TO ME.

YOU WANT ME TO GO TO HOLY DONUT AND GET YOU A COFFEE?

OH, THAT WOULD BE AWFULLY SWEET OF YOU.

CAN YOU GET ME A BEAR CLAW, TOO?

YOU *ARE* DEPRESSED.

WEAR YOUR HAT!

NOTHING TO DO... IT'S UP TO YOU...

SGT. PEPPER'S ONE AND ONLY LONELY HEARTS CLUB BAND...

Z

KISS

NEW YEAR

I'M SO PROUD OF YOU, BUNNYBEAR.

THANK YOU FOR COMING!

ARE YOU KIDDING ME? I WOULDN'T MISS THIS!

WHEN PEOPLE START TO ARRIVE, SEND THEM IN FOR COFFEE AND COCOA AND OTHER GOODIES.

I THINK I NEED TO USE THE BATHROOM REAL QUICK.

YOU'RE NOT ALLOWED TO PANIC.

TWO SONGS, RUPA. WE TOTALLY GOT THIS.

SHE'LL BE OKAY.

SHE GETS LIKE THIS BEFORE TESTS AND STUFF, SHE JUST HAS TO DO HER BREATHING EXERCISES.

VVRRM

WHERE'S RUPA?

SHE JUST WENT INSIDE FOR A MINUTE.

ACTUALLY, IF YOU WANT TO GO IN, THERE'S FOOD AND DRINKS.

WHAT KIND OF FOOD?

HUSH.

SKREEEE

E ABOUT BIO DIESEL

WHERE'RE MOM AND DAD?

I GUESS THEY'RE STILL AT THEIR MEETING.

HOW MUCH CAN PEOPLE POSSIBLY HAVE TO SAY ABOUT WATER QUALITY?

DID YOU SEE ALL THOSE CHARTS AND GRAPHS DAD MADE?

THERE'S COFFEE INSIDE IF YOU WANT.

?

?

?

HI, GIRLS!

THIS IS SO EXCITING!

RRRRRRR...

OH MY GOD.

WHO'RE YOU GUYS?

OH, I'M PETE, AND...

...UM, THIS IS MY INTERN, CONNOR.

AND YOU KNOW ME.

HEY, IS YOUR BAND CALLED HAPPY NEW YEAR?

NO.

THAT WOULD BE KIND OF COOL, ACTUALLY.

YEAH.

?!

HI, UM, EXCUSE ME...

BUT BEFORE WE PLAY OUR NEXT SONG, I HAVE AN ANNOUNCEMENT TO MAKE. I'VE DEFERRED MY ACCEPTANCE TO PARK ACADEMY...

...SO I WON'T BE SKIPPING EIGHTH GRADE AFTER ALL. (WHEW)

MOM, PLEASE DON'T FREAK OUT... I CAN TAKE HONORS ADVANCED ALGEBRA AND AP BIO AT HILLTOP TECH.

WHAT? IT'S ALMOST TIME.

FIVE, FOUR, THREE, TWO, ONE!

HAPPY NEW YEAR!

Smack
Smack

G'NIGHT.

YAWN

THEY WEREN'T HOLDING HANDS OR ANYTHING, SO MAYBE...

BUT, I MEAN, THEY'RE THE PERFECT COUPLE.

...

BOTH OF THEIR NAMES EVEN START WITH C.

I KEEP TELLING YOU, YOU'RE FRIENDS WITH CAMILLE, SO JUST ASK HER. LIKE, RIGHT NOW— CALL HER, TEXT HER, WHATEVER.

THAT WOULD BE SO OBVIOUS.

! FWAP

AND DID YOU NOTICE HOW VANESSA SANG? LIKE THE WORDS WERE HERS?

AND SHE...

munch munch

 I USED TO BE CRUEL TO MY WOMAN...

 THAT VERSE ALWAYS BOTHERS ME.

 YEAH, ME, TOO.

WHAT DOES HE MEAN?

 IT'S A PAUL SONG, BUT JOHN SAID THAT BIT WAS ABOUT HIM.

 REALLY?

 YEAH, HE HAD THIS CHIP ON HIS SHOULDER WHEN HE WAS YOUNG. IT WAS PART OF HIS WHOLE AGGRESSIVE, TEDDY BOY ATTITUDE.

 HE WAS ANGRY AND GOT IN A LOT OF FIGHTS, AND WITH WOMEN, HE WAS VIOLENT AT TIMES.

 I KNOW IT'S HARD TO HEAR.

YEAH.

WHAT'S A TEDDY BOY?

"EDWARDIAN" DRAPE JACKET →

" THE TEDS WERE YOUNG GUYS IN ENGLAND IN THE FIFTIES. THEY DRESSED IN AN OLD-FASHIONED KIND OF WAY AND WERE INTO ROCK 'N' ROLL ..."

"... AND THEY HAD A REAL REPUTATION FOR BEING DANGEROUS."

TED—FROM "EDWARDIAN"

← DRAINPIPE TROUSERS

BROTHEL CREEPERS ↓

"IN THE FIFTIES, THERE WERE THE TEDS, AND THEN IN THE SIXTIES, THERE WERE THE MODS, WHO HAD A STYLE OF THEIR OWN."

"THEY RODE AROUND ON SCOOTERS AND LISTENED TO SOUL MUSIC."

"THEN AFTER THE MODS, THERE WERE THE PUNKS..."

SCRATCH

BUT, I DIGRESS.

I JUST CAN'T BELIEVE THAT ABOUT JOHN.

I KNOW.

IT'S AWFUL, AND I WISH IT WEREN'T TRUE. JOHN WAS THE FIRST TO ACKNOWLEDGE THAT HE WAS A VERY FLAWED MAN.

HE DID LATER APOLOGIZE FOR HIS BEHAVIOR. HE SAID THAT HE WANTED TO TRY TO MAKE AMENDS.

YOU LOOK AWFUL, DAD. ARE YOU OKAY?

SORT OF.

I'M UP AND DOWN, BUT BETTER THAN I WAS LAST WEEK. YOU WERE RIGHT— IT WAS HARD SEEING YOUR MOM.

YOU NEED ANOTHER HOBBY OR, LIKE, SOMETHING NEW IN YOUR LIFE.

GOOD ADVICE, KIDDO. THANK YOU.

MAYBE YOU NEED A HUG?

DEFINITELY.

♪♪♪♪ IT'S GETTING BETTER ALL THE TIME ♪♪♪♪ ♪♪♪ ♪

SKITCH
SKETCH

HEY, LUCY! INCOMING!

CAN I TALK TO YOU FOR A SEC?

THE GOOD NEWS IS THAT CAMILLE AND CONNOR ARE JUST FRIENDS.

...

WHAT'S THE BAD NEWS?

VANESSA ASKED TREVOR TO TALK TO CONNOR...

I DIDN'T TELL HER TO, I SWEAR.

CONNOR SAID THAT HE LIKES US BOTH—I MEAN, ME AND YOU...

BUT YOU'RE JUST A LITTLE YOUNG, YOU KNOW?

YOUNG?

YOU JUST TURNED TWELVE.

THREE MONTHS AGO.

I'LL BE THIRTEEN IN MARCH.

SO?

THE FOUR OF US ARE GONNA HANG OUT THIS WEEKEND.

WAIT— WHAT?

ME AND CONNOR AND VANESSA AND TREVOR.

YOU HATE VANESSA.

I DON'T *HATE* HER.

WHATEVER.

I GUESS I'LL SEE YOU AT LUNCH?

KNOCK
KNOCK

LUCY!
HELLO!

DO I SEEM YOUNG TO YOU?

WELL, BUNNY, I'M SEVENTY-THREE YEARS OLD. TO ME, YOU'RE A BABY.

BUT DO I SEEM YOUNGER THAN MY FRIENDS?

NOT THAT I'VE NOTICED.

I DIDN'T KNOW YOU HAD A CANE.

IT'S MY NEW FAVORITE ACCESSORY.

CAN I GET YOU ANYTHING?
ARE YOU HUNGRY?
NO, I JUST WANNA SIT HERE FOR A WHILE.

ALL YOU NEED IS LOVE.
WHAT A BIG LIE THAT IS!

I SUPPOSE LOVE CAN MAKE THINGS DIFFICULT SOMETIMES.

I WISH I NEVER LOVED ANYONE.

HOW OLD IS MOM HERE?

MAYBE THIRTEEN OR FOURTEEN.

SIGH

YOU WANNA TELL ME WHAT THIS IS ALL ABOUT?
DEMAND L'IMPOSS

THANK YOU, PAPA.

THANK YOU.

I'M FREEZING!

ME, TOO!

giggle

SHARP CUTS

HEY!

MISS EMILY! RYAN!

?!

WHO'RE THEY?

MY DAD'S CRUSH AND HER SON.

HOW'RE YOU, LUCY?

I'M ALL RIGHT.

NICE HAIRCUT!

IT'S TOO SHORT, AND NOW MY FACE LOOKS ALL DIFFERENT.

YOU HAVE CHOCOLATE ON YOUR FACE.

WIPE

BETTER?

YEAH.

KICK

OH, THIS IS MY FRIEND RUPA.

GOOD TO MEET YOU.

YOU GUYS SHOULD COME OVER FOR DINNER SOMETIME THIS WEEK.

MY DAD'S AN EXCELLENT COOK.

HE IS. I CAN VOUCH FOR THAT.

I DON'T KNOW, I ...

DAD AND I WERE JUST TALKING ABOUT YOU THE OTHER DAY.

YOU WERE?

I'LL TELL HIM TO GIVE YOU A CALL. DOES HE HAVE YOUR NUMBER?

HOW DOES IT FEEL TO BE ONE OF THE BEAUTIFUL PEOPLE...

?

!!!

WHAT'RE YOU DOING?!

WAITING FOR YOU.

BABY YOU'RE A RICH MAN...

BEST SONG ON THIS ALBUM.

NO, IT'S NOT.

ARE YOU KIDDING?

"RINGO'S DRUMS NEVER SOUNDED BETTER!"

HOW WAS YOUR DATE?

TERRIBLE.

Flip Flip

I'M SORRY. I SHOULDN'T HAVE DITCHED YOU LIKE THAT.

FOR WHAT IT'S WORTH, I DON'T THINK CONNOR WAS THAT INTERESTED IN EITHER OF US.

BASICALLY, TREVOR AND I WATCHED VANESSA AND CONNOR HANG OUT FOR TWO HOURS.

IT WAS BRILLIANT ON VANESSA'S PART— YOU KNOW, TWO BIRDS, ONE STONE.

HAVE YOU ALWAYS HAD THAT?

UNICORNS against NUCLEAR WAR

YUP. IT WAS MY MOM'S.

SIGH SO, YOU'RE, LIKE, MY ONLY FRIEND.

I'M NOT.

YOU'RE MY BEST FRIEND.

OKAY, I'M GONNA GO HOME NOW.

YOU CAN STAY IF YOU WANT.

I SHOULD GO. CHARLES IS IN THE MIDDLE OF A STAR WARS MARATHON.

HIS GIRLFRIEND BROKE UP WITH HIM.

HIS ONLINE GIRLFRIEND?

THE ONE AND ONLY. THEY HADN'T EVEN MET IN PERSON AND SHE NEEDED MORE SPACE.

OUCH.

TOMORROW'S THE DEADLINE TO ENTER THE TALENT SHOW TRYOUTS.

WE HAVE TO *TRY OUT*?

SORT OF. THEY REALLY JUST WANNA MAKE SURE NOBODY DOES ANYTHING TOO SCANDALOUS.

OR WEARS ANYTHING TOO SCANDALOUS. WE HAVE TO TRY OUT "IN COSTUME."

SO MUCH FOR FREEDOM OF EXPRESSION.

WHEN ARE THE TRYOUTS?

END OF FEBRUARY. THE TALENT SHOW'S THE FRIDAY BEFORE SPRING BREAK.

WANNA ENTER? YOU CAN DO YOUR MAGIC TRICKS, AND I'LL BE YOUR LOVELY ASSISTANT!

FOR THE GRAND FINALE, YOU CAN MAKE ME DISAPPEAR, AND THEN I CAN TAKE A FEW WEEKS OFF SCHOOL BEFORE FABULOUSLY REAPPEARING IN TIME FOR SUMMER.

I SOLD MY MAGIC KIT A YEAR AGO.

TRAGIC!

EIGHTY-THREE AND A HALF.

WE HAVE TO DECIDE ON A NAME.

STRAWBERRY JAM.

YOU WANNA TALK TO VANESSA ABOUT IT?

NOT REALLY.

CAMILLE SITS WITH YOU GUYS, LIKE, EVERY DAY NOW.

ALL THEY TALK ABOUT IS CONNOR.

YOU KNOW, CAMILLE SHOULD ACTUALLY BE IN NINTH GRADE, BUT SHE GOT HELD BACK IN KINDERGARTEN.

APPARENTLY SHE WAS A BITER.

GOOD TO KNOW.

CAN WE JUST PUT "TO BE DETERMINED"?

WHAT IF THEY THINK THAT'S OUR NAME?

FINE.

YOU HAVE A BETTER NAME?

STRAWBERRY JAM SOUNDS TOO JUVENILE. I'M NOT THE ONLY ONE WHO THINKS SO.

ARE YOU REFERRING TO YOUR MATURE FRIEND?

WHO CLEARLY HAS SUCH DISCERNING TASTE?

SHUT UP!

BITE ME.

OR HAVE YOU OUTGROWN THAT LITTLE HABIT?

COOKIE'S USING A CANE NOW.

YOUR DAD TOLD ME.

SO, IS THAT A NO?

I'LL THINK ABOUT IT.

WE COULD VISIT LIVERPOOL AND TAKE THE FERRY ACROSS THE MERSEY.

ACROSS THE WHAT?

THE MERSEY RIVER.

FERRY 'CROSS THE MERSEY...

TAP TAP

BY GERRY AND THE PACEMAKERS.

THEY WERE ANOTHER LIVERPUDLIAN BAND, PART OF THE MERSEY-BEAT.

MERSEY BEAT

Beatles

Top Poll

CAN I ASK YOU A PERSONAL QUESTION? HOW OLD WERE YOU WHEN YOU FIRST FELL IN LOVE?

REALLY FELL IN LOVE? PROBABLY ABOUT SEVENTEEN.

DOES IT COUNT IF THE PERSON YOU LOVE DOESN'T FALL IN LOVE WITH YOU?

I SUPPOSE SO. HOW DID YOU KNOW WHEN YOU DIDN'T LOVE DAD ANYMORE?

ÇEŞME IZMIR

A PART OF ME WILL ALWAYS LOVE YOUR DAD.

SO I'M ALWAYS GOING TO HAVE THIS FEELING INSIDE ME?

NO, IT'LL FADE OVER TIME. IT'S COMPLICATED, SWEETHEART.

ELEANOR? OKAY. OKAY.

DON'T WORRY. I'LL BE RIGHT THERE.

I'M REALLY SORRY ABOUT THIS. I HAVE TO GO.

MY MOTHER-IN-LAW... EX-MOTHER-IN-LAW...

I'M SURE SHE'S FINE, BUT SHE'S HAVING TROUBLE, UM...

I'M GOING WITH YOU.

WE JUST HAVE TO WALK IN THERE LIKE WE DON'T CARE.

(SIGH) ALL RIGHT.

YOU READY?

DO WE HAVE TO DO THIS TODAY? I MEAN IT'S—

I DON'T BELIEVE IN VALENTINE'S DAY. GREETING CARD COMPANIES TURNED IT INTO THIS BIG, STUPID THING, AND IT'S A HUGE WASTE OF PAPER.

WHEN D'YOU THINK BEN FRANKLIN WILL BE BACK?

I DUNNO. C'MON, CAN WE JUST GET THIS OVER WITH?

REMEMBER, SAY HI LIKE NOTHING HAPPENED.

NOTHING DID HAPPEN.

GEORGIE AND GEORGIE'S FRIEND! IT'S BEEN A WHILE.

MY NAME IS LUCY.

I GUESS THE INTERN HAS AN INTERN NOW.

HOW'S IT GOING?

GREAT, REALLY GREAT.

YOU'RE ACTING WEIRD.

I DIDN'T KNOW *SHE* WAS GONNA BE HERE.

LET'S JUST GO.

IS YOUR BROTHER STILL A WRECK OVER THAT GIRL HE NEVER MET?

HE'S A WRECK IN GENERAL.

I'LL GIVE HIM A CALL. SEE IF I CAN GET HIM OUT OF HIS ROOM.

GOOD LUCK WITH THAT.

DON'T BE A STRANGER.

OKAY, BYE.

BYE!

SEE YA.

HOW CAN YOU BE FRIENDS WITH HER?

WE JUST ALWAYS HAVE BEEN, LIKE, SINCE PRESCHOOL. I CAN'T REMEMBER NOT BEING HER FRIEND.

SHE'S NOT SO BAD. SHE JUST NEVER BACKS DOWN FROM A FIGHT.

SNIFF SNIFF

WHILE MY GUITAR GENTLY WEEPS...

Sob *Sob* *Sob*

ANY DINNER REQUESTS?

SWEETHEART, WHAT'S WRONG?

GEORGE IS DEAD.

LUCE, HE'S BEEN DEAD FOR A LONG TIME NOW.

I KNOW, BUT I NEVER REALLY FELT IT BEFORE... AND IT'S LIKE, I'M JUST GETTING TO KNOW HIM.

GEORGE HAD A BIG *SOUL*, DIDN'T HE?

"I REMEMBER WATCHING THE NEWS THE DAY HE DIED AND GETTING SO DEPRESSED. EVEN THE CAT SEEMED SAD."

THAT WAS BEFORE MONKEY?

YEAH, WE STILL HAD TILLY. YOU TWO DIDN'T GET ALONG VERY WELL.

WHY NOT?

"WHEN YOU SHOWED UP, TILLY WAS OLD, AND YOU WERE NEW AND LOUD AND GOT ALL THE ATTENTION."

"BUT SHE PUT UP WITH YOU."

IT'S NOT FAIR. I MEAN, THE ROLLING STONES STAYED TOGETHER. THE BEACH BOYS STAYED MORE OR LESS TOGETHER. FLEETWOOD MAC SORT OF STAYED TOGETHER.

"WHAT IF THE BEATLES HAD NEVER BROKEN UP AND EVERYTHING WAS DIFFERENT?"

"THEN I COULD GROW UP AND BECOME THE FIFTH BEATLE..."

SHOULD WE TRY IT ONCE MORE?

NO.

I WROTE A SONG—I MEAN, JUST THE WORDS.

LUCY WRITES OUR LYRICS.

WHAT—IS THAT A RULE?

NO.

"I WANNA KISS YOU FOREVER"?

THAT'S JUST... YUCK!

HEY, TOO BAD YOU'RE NOT STILL KISSING TREVOR. THEN YOU COULD RHYME TREVOR WITH FOREVER.

WE'RE BIG KIDS NOW—KISSING ISN'T YUCKY ANYMORE...

NOT THAT YOU'D KNOW...

THERE SHOULD BE A HORROR MOVIE WHERE PEOPLE CAN'T STOP KISSING AND EVENTUALLY SUFFOCATE EACH OTHER.

I GUESS I'D BE BITTER, TOO, IF NOBODY LOVED ME.

239

SO, RUPA HAD THIS IDEA.

WHAT?

OUR NAME IS FOR SURE STRAWBERRY JAM— VANESSA EVEN AGREED...

BUT...

THIS WEEK, RUPA'S GOING TO TRY TO WRITE SOME MUSIC FOR VANESSA'S SONG.

I'M NOT PLAYING IT AT THE TALENT SHOW.

WE HAVEN'T REALLY FIGURED THAT OUT YET...

WELL, I'M JUST SAYING.

WHAT IS IT?

RROWLL

YOU WANNA HEAR YOUR SONG?

SKKKRTCH

COME ON, COME ON...

CHRISTOPHER PLUMMER

EVERYBODY'S GOT SOMETHING TO HIDE EXCEPT FOR ME AND MY MONKEY!

MEOW!

I WANT YOU TO GO ON THAT TRIP TO LONDON NEXT MONTH.

I'M FINE, BUNNY. MY COUGH IS CLEARING UP AND I CAN GET UP AND DOWN STAIRS WITHOUT USING MY INHALER. BESIDES, YOUR DAD WILL BE HERE.

HAVE YOU BEEN TO LONDON?

MY FRIEND SUSAN AND I HOPPED THE POND THE SUMMER AFTER WE GRADUATED FROM COLLEGE.

I THOUGHT YOU WENT TO PARIS?

"FIRST WE WENT TO LONDON. I REMEMBER WALKING DOWN CARNABY STREET, FEELING SO YOUNG AND POWERFUL, LIKE MY HEART WOULD JUST GROW BIGGER AND BIGGER AND NEVER STOP BEATING. I COULD MAKE MYSELF BELIEVE THAT SOMEWHERE NEARBY, GEORGE WAS QUIETLY LISTENING — THAT THE SOUND OF MY HEART WOULD PULL HIM TOWARD ME, AND WE WOULD LIVE HAPPILY EVER AFTER."

WOW.

ONCE UPON A TIME, I WAS TWENTY-ONE YEARS OLD.

GEORGE DIDN'T FIND YOU?

NOPE.

JOHN

"HE WAS PROBABLY HANGING OUT IN INDIA WITH THE MAHARISHI AND PRUDENCE FARROW."

SO SUSAN AND I WENT TO PARIS, AND I FOUND ALBERT.

DO YOU HAVE ANY TWOS?

NOPE. GO FISH.

HOW MANY DATES HAVE THEY BEEN ON NOW?

THIS IS THE THIRD.

MY DAD GOT HIS HAIR CUT AND BOUGHT A NEW TIE.

THEY'RE PROBABLY FALLING IN LOVE.

MY MOM'S IN LOVE WITH ME!

SHE LOVES YOU, SILLY. SHE'S NOT *IN LOVE* WITH YOU!

WHAT'S THE DIFFERENCE?

A LOT!

IT'S YOUR TURN.

ALL RIGHT.

GOT ANY NINES?

ANY KINGS?

NOPE. GO FISH.

I'M THINKING ABOUT HAVING A BIRTHDAY PARTY.

YOU TOTALLY SHOULD.

DO YOU HAVE ANY...

ACES?

GO FISH!

WHO AM I GONNA INVITE? YOU AND RUPA?

AND MAYA AND KATE? WE COULD HAVE A SLUMBER PARTY...

CAN I COME?

YEAH, SURE.

I HAVEN'T HAD A BIRTHDAY PARTY SINCE I WAS YOUR AGE.

WHY?

"MY SIXTH BIRTHDAY WAS A DISASTER. MY MOM HAD TO CRITICIZE EVERY GIFT I OPENED..."

MORE PLASTIC, AND PROBABLY MADE IN CHINA, TOO.

HONG KONG.

AND SHE FROSTED THE CAKE WITH THIS ORGANIC, FAIR TRADE CHOCOLATE THAT WASN'T EVEN SWEET.

GIMME YOUR KINGS.

DON'T YOU THINK YOU SHOULD INVITE VANESSA?

UH, NO. YOU THINK SHE'D INVITE ME TO HER BIRTHDAY?

ANY FIVES?

CAN WE WATCH THE MOVIE NOW?

BUT I'M WINNING!

I CONCEDE.

ME, TOO.

THAT MEANS YOU ALREADY WON.

I DID?

I'M THE WINNER!

♪ ♪ ♪ ♫
WE ALL LIVE IN A YELLOW SUBMARINE...

Clik

BOOM BA BOO
TAP TAP TAP

SAIL THE SHIP...
BOMP-PA BOM...

CHOP THE TREE...

ALL TOGETHER NOW...

ALLTOGETHERNOW...

HEY!

ALL TOGETHER NOW

I WANNA DO MY SONG AGAIN!

WE GOT THROUGH IT ONCE.

BUT WE DID YOUR SONG THREE TIMES!

IT'S NOT MY SONG. LUCY WROTE THE LYRICS.

YEAH, RIGHT. YOU PROBABLY DICTATED THEM TO HER.

SHE DID NOT!

SHUT UP, LUCY!

YOU SHUT UP!

TRY AND MAKE ME.

YOUR SONG SUCKS, LITERALLY.

YOU SUCK!

SHUT UP!

248

TO SEE
PHAROAH SANDERS
PERFORM?

YOU'RE THE ADULT—
YOU FIGURE IT OUT!

FINE.

RIIING-

I'M AFRAID THERE'S
BEEN A SLIGHT
CHANGE OF PLAN.

IS EVERYTHING
OKAY?

LUCY'S, UH,
NOT HERSELF.

YES, I AM!
I'M EXACTLY MYSELF!

I CAN THROW SOMETHING
TOGETHER FOR DINNER
AND WE CAN HANG OUT
HERE.

YOU WERE LOOKING
FORWARD TO PHAROAH.

OH, WELL.

YOU LOOK BEAUTIFUL,
BY THE WAY.

NO KISSING!

THIS IS NICE.

300 PIECES PUZZLE

YEAH.

YOU'RE WORRIED ABOUT LUCY?

CAN I GO SAY HI TO HER?

I'M NOT SURE SHE'S FIT FOR COMPANY, BUDDY.

YOU CAN TALK TO ME — IF YOU'RE LONELY YOU CAN TALK TO ME...

HEY, BULLDOG ...

TAP TAP

I HAVE TO TELL YOU SOMETHING.

NOW WHAT?

VANESSA AND CAMILLE ARE STARTING THEIR OWN BAND.

JUST THE TWO OF THEM?

AND A DRUM MACHINE.

OUCH.

HOW D'YOU ALWAYS KNOW EVERYTHING?

I LISTEN, AND I USED TO BE A MAGICIAN, SO I SORT OF KNOW HOW TO MAKE MYSELF INVISIBLE, OR AT LEAST, LESS VISIBLE.

WHAT'S THE BIG NEWS THIS AFTERNOON, KATE?

UM.

NOTHING.

CAN I HAVE A PIECE OF GUM?

BEEP

HMM. LET ME THINK ABOUT THAT.

ARE YOU STILL THINKING?

YES, VERY DEEPLY.

CLIK CLIK

IF I CAN GET RUPA BACK, THEN WE JUST NEED A SINGER.

DON'T LOOK AT ME. MY VOICE RETIRED AFTER LAST YEAR'S TALENT SHOW.

HEY, MAYA.

HEY, YOURSELF.

CAN YOU SING?

252

CAN I? ...OR WILL I?

WILL YOU? FOR OUR BAND... PLEASE?

NO.

WHY NOT?

SEVEN TWENTY-FIVE AN HOUR, MINIMUM WAGE.

WE DON'T HAVE THAT MUCH MON— GOT ANYTHING YOU COULD SELL OR TRADE?

MAYBE A GUITAR... OR A SCOOTER... I HAVE A COMPLETE COLLECTION OF FUNNY BUNNIES.

GOOD FOR YOU. WHAT KIND OF SCOOTER? A RAZOR, HARDLY USED AT ALL.

DOES IT COME WITH A HELMET? UH, SURE.

DEAL.

I FEEL DIRTY.

spring

WHAT IS IT ABOUT THAT COVER? I USED TO STARE AT IT FOR HOURS.

WHY'S JOHN ALL IN WHITE? WHY ISN'T PAUL WEARING ANY SHOES?

"WHY'S RINGO'S COAT SO AWESOME?"

PEOPLE HAVE COME UP WITH THEORIES FOR EVERY LITTLE DETAIL.

http://www.numbernine.org   🔍 Paul is dead

THE GREAT PAUL is DEAD HOAX

TOP PAUL IS DEAD CLUES

ABBEY ROAD

○ PAUL IS BAREFOOT ~ many cultures aroun world bury their dead barefoot.
○ 28IF ~ the license plate on the car near G reads 28IF, meaning Paul would have been 28 old if he was still alive.
TAP TAP TAP TAP CLICK

A BUNCH OF CRAPOLA.

I MEAN, I KNOW IT'S POSED OR PLANNED, OR WHATEVER, BUT IT SEEMS LIKE SUCH A REAL MOMENT IN TIME.

I CAN'T EXPLAIN...

HAVE YOU LISTENED TO IT YET?

NO.

YOU GOTTA LISTEN TO IT ALL THE WAY THROUGH. IT'S JUST ABOUT PERFECT, AS AN *ALBUM*, A COMPLETE ENTITY.

NOBODY APPRECIATES THE BEAUTY OF AN ALBUM ANYMORE. IPODS, PANDORA, SPOTIFY— WE'RE DEGENERATING INTO A SHUFFLE CULTURE.

NO RESPECT FOR THE MUSIC.

HOW'D YOUR CONVERSATION WITH RUPA GO?

SHE SAID SHE'LL COME BACK, BUT ONLY FOR A TRIAL. SHE WANTS TO SEE HOW THINGS GO.

SHE'S GOT A GOOD HEART, THAT RUPA.

I GUESS.

SO, ARE YOU IN LOVE WITH EMILY?

HA HA.

WHAT?

I LIKE HER VERY MUCH, BUT WE'RE JUST GETTING TO KNOW EACH OTHER, LUCE.

SOME PEOPLE FALL IN LOVE AT FIRST SIGHT.

THAT'S INFATUATION.

BUT, COOKIE AND ALBERT?

OKAY, I SUPPOSE IN CERTAIN SITUATIONS THINGS MIRACULOUSLY ALIGN, AND THERE'S THIS MUTUAL, SIMULTANEOUS RECOGNITION, SO MUCH BIGGER THAN A SPARK.

YES

JOHN LENNON MEETS YOKO ONO. INDICA GALLERY, 1966

ETERNAL ROMANTIC.

(SIGH) COOKIE LIKES TO TALK ABOUT HER DAYS AS A REVOLUTIONARY, BUT IN MY OPINION, HER DECISION TO COME HOME AND RAISE A CHILD BY HERSELF, WITHOUT AN OUNCE OF SHAME OR REGRET, IS WHAT TRULY MAKES HER A REVOLUTIONARY.

?

BACK THEN, EVEN DIVORCE WAS STILL SOMEWHAT TABOO — AN UNMARRIED MOTHER WHO DIDN'T NEED OR WANT A MAN TO SUPPORT HER WAS SOMETHING ELSE ALL TOGETHER.

VIVA LA REVOLUCIÓN!

chomp

munch
munch
munch

... SO NOW MAYA'S IN OUR BAND, AND EVEN THOUGH THE DEADLINE WAS LAST MONTH ...

... PRINCIPAL BLAIR'S LETTING VANESSA AND CAMILLE ENTER THE TALENT SHOW ...

... AND LAST NIGHT, WE HAD TO TAKE COOKIE TO THE HOSPITAL, BECAUSE HER PNEUMONITIS GOT WORSE AGAIN ...

... SHE HAS TO SLEEP WITH AN OXYGEN MASK ...

wipe

I'M GLAD YOU'RE BACK.

yawn

IT'S JUST ... IT'S BEEN A LONG, COLD, LONELY WINTER.

DO·DO·DO·DO

SOMETIMES I DON'T KNOW HOW ...

LET EACH FOLLOWING DAY CORRECT THE LAST.

260

BUT THERE ARE SO MANY TERRIBLE THINGS THAT CAN'T BE UNDONE.

DEMANDEZ L'IMPOSSIBLE

DECEMBER, 1980

MILLIONS MOURNED THE TRAGIC DEATH OF JOHN LENNON TODAY —

THE YOUNG AND THE MIDDLE-AGED SHARED A SENSE OF GRIEF OVER THE INEXPLICABLE SLAYING OF LENNON, MURDERED BY A YOUNG MAN WHO'D BEEN A FAN OF HIS AND THE BEATLES FOR THE LAST FIFTEEN YEARS.

THE KILLING TOOK PLACE LAST NIGHT AS LENNON AND HIS WIFE, YOKO ONO, WERE ENTERING THEIR MANHATTAN APARTMENT BUILDING...

LUCY!

I GOTTA GO.

MROW!

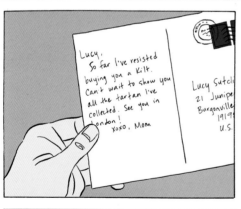

Lucy,
So far I've resisted buying you a kilt. Can't wait to show you all the tartan I've collected. See you in London!
xoxo, Mom

Lucy Sutcli[ff]
21 Junipe[r]
Burgonville[,]
1919[?]
U.S.

GREETINGS FROM
St. Kilda, Scotland
STAC AN ARMIN

ONCE THERE WAS A WAY TO GET BACK HOMEWARD...

WELCOME TO OUR LITTLE CORNER OF THE WORLD.

I'M SURE THE VIEW'S NOT ALL THAT DIFFERENT.

YOU'D BE SURPRISED.

I CAN'T STAND TO LISTEN TO THEM ANYMORE.

CONNOR SAYS THIS AND CONNOR SAYS THAT.

DID YOU FIND OUT ANYTHING ABOUT THEIR BAND, LIKE *WHAT* THEY'RE PRACTICING OR *WHEN* THEY'RE PRACTICING?

NOPE.

HAVE YOU HEARD ANYTHING?

THEY'RE CALLING THEMSELVES NOBODY'S FAULT, SO THEY CAN SAY, *HI, WE'RE NOBODY'S FAULT.*

Chuckle

D'YOU THINK YOU COULD TRY TO FIND OUT MORE?

I DON'T KNOW. ALL OF THIS SPYING IS GIVING ME A HEADACHE.

MY LIFE IS A HEADACHE.

...

my life is a headache

263

D'YOU THINK I SHOULD TEXT HER AGAIN?

NO.

ARE YOU SURE YOU CAN'T SING?

VERY.

DON'T LOOK AT ME.

BUT YOU COULD BE A 21ST CENTURY KAREN CARPENTER, MINUS THE TRAGEDY.

YOU'RE LATE.

CANDY CRUSH. I GOT TO LEVEL 503.

THAT'S GREAT.

POP

YOU WANT SOMETHING TO DRINK?

NAH. THANKS, THOUGH.

YOU KNOW THE SONG "TWIST AND SHOUT," RIGHT?

IS THAT THE SCOOTER?

YUP. ALMOST NEW. THE HELMET, UH ...

IT'S PERFECT.

IT IS?

FOR MY LITTLE SISTER.

HER BIKE GOT STOLEN.

OH.

IF I LET YOU TAKE IT TODAY, HOW DO WE KNOW YOU'LL KEEP COMING TO PRACTICE?

I GIVE YOU MY WORD.

I TRUST YOU.

LUCY!

SO, THE BEATLES, HUH?

ACTUALLY, "TWIST AND SHOUT" WAS ORIGINALLY A HIT BY THE ISLEY BROTHERS.

WHATEVER.

TWIST AND SHOUT...

COME ON, COME ON, COME ON, BABY NOW...

I HOPE YOU DON'T EXPECT ME TO, LIKE, DANCE AROUND.

!!

!!

HOW'S IT GOING, KIDDOS?

265

JUST COULDN'T STAY AWAY, COULD YOU?

I HAPPEN TO LIVE IN THIS NEIGHBORHOOD.

GOD, SO MUCH DRAMA!

MAYBE WE SHOULD PRACTICE WITH THE GARAGE DOORS SHUT.

I GUESS SO.

SO THEY'RE UP FIRST, AND THEY PLAY "TWIST AND SHOUT," WHICH VANESSA KNEW *WE* WERE GOING TO PLAY—

BUT THEY PLAY IT SUPER FAST, LIKE PUNKED UP. IF THEY HAD A DRUMMER, THEY'D BE LEGITIMATE.

I MEAN, IT WAS LIKE THE FIRST SONG WE LEARNED, SO IT'S SOLID.

(SIGH) CAN YOU BELIEVE IT?

GOOD THING IT WAS JUST THE TRYOUTS, HUH?

THEN IT WAS LIKE THEY WERE STARING AT US THE WHOLE TIME WE PLAYED, LIKE, WITH PITY...

LIKE THEY WERE SAYING TO US, "OH, YOU GUYS ARE SO CUTE AND SINCERE."

I'M SORRY, BUNNY.

DID I MENTION THAT MAYA SINGS LIKE A NARCOLEPTIC?

WELL, MAYBE WE COULD LOAD HER UP ON SUGAR? I COULD BAKE MY FAMOUS COFFEE CAKE.

IT'S JUST THAT SHE DOESN'T CARE.

WHEN DO I GET TO MEET YOUR NEW LADY FRIEND, DANIEL?

WILL YOU TELL ME ANOTHER STORY ABOUT ALBERT?

SURE.

Sip

YOUR GRANDFATHER WAS A BIT OF A THIEF.

HE LIKED TO *COLLECT* THINGS, AS HE USED TO SAY—NOTHING BIG, JUST LITTLE TOKENS.

THE NIGHT WE MET, HE PLUCKED A SINGLE STRAND OF MY HAIR AND PUT IT IN HIS POCKET.

LATER, HE POCKETED MY FAVORITE FINGERNAIL POLISH.

I'D FIND STUFF IN HIS ROOM—A CUP FROM CAFÉ DE FLORE, A MENU FROM MAXIM'S...

I DARE YOU TO KNOCK ON MY BROTHER'S DOOR, AND IF HE ANSWERS, ASK HIM FOR A HUG.

A HUG?

I DON'T KNOW—IT SEEMS SWEETER AND MORE INTIMATE THAN A KISS.

!

AAAAAGGGHH!

AAAADAAAAGGGHHHH!

WHO'S THAT?

OKAY, FROM NOW ON, YOU'RE ONLY ALLOWED TO SCREAM LIKE THAT IF SOMEBODY'S MURDERING YOU...

!!!

YOU WEREN'T INVITED.

I DON'T CARE ABOUT YOUR STUPID PARTY.

!! OOFH

WHAT'RE YOU...

DOES THAT COUNT?

DID YOU GET MY TEXTS?

MY PHONE'S IN MY BAG. I MUST HAVE IT ON VIBRATE.

TYPICAL.

WHAT IS IT?

FINE, YOU CAN COME IN.

SHE CAME IN THROUGH THE BEDROOM WINDOW.

I DIDN'T WANT TO RING THE DOORBELL THIS LATE, AND I SAW YOUR LIGHT ON.

WHAT TIME IS IT?

TEN AFTER TWELVE.

I'VE NEVER BEEN UP THIS LATE BEFORE!

HAPPY BIRTHDAY.

YEAH, THANKS.

DID YOU KNOW THAT CONNOR AND CAMILLE USED TO GO OUT?

NO.

NO.

THEY WERE TOGETHER FOR YEARS. I MEAN, SHE'S KNOWN HIM SO MUCH LONGER THAN I HAVE. IT'S NOT FAIR.

ARE YOU KIDDING ME?

I JUST, I FEEL LIKE THEY'VE BOTH BEEN LYING TO ME. (SOB)

(SIGH)

LOOK, HE'S OBVIOUSLY SUPER INTO YOU, SO WHAT'S THE PROBLEM?

SNAP OUT OF IT, ALL RIGHT?

GIVE HER A PIECE OF CANDY OR SOMETHING.

KNOCK
KNOCK

HOW'S MY GIRL?

OKAY, I GUESS?

YOU'RE HURT...

DON'T BE SILLY. I'M JUST WORN OUT.

I THINK I BETTER CALL DAD.

I HAVE SOMETHING FOR YOU, FROM YOUR GRANDFATHER.

I SPENT THE LAST WEEK LOOKING EVERYWHERE FOR IT...
OOPH
!

AND THEN I FINALLY FOUND IT, RIGHT IN THE TOP DRAWER OF MY BEDSIDE TABLE.

HIS HARMONICA.
L'IMPOSSIBL
I TOOK IT THE NIGHT I LEFT... I NEVER TOLD ANYONE, NOT EVEN YOUR MOTHER.

SO YOU WERE A THIEF, TOO?

I WON'T TELL ANYONE. I PROMISE.

DEMAND L'IMPOSSI
WOULD YOU GET ME A GLASS OF WATER, SWEETHEART? I NEED TO TAKE SOME PILLS.

271

HERE.

I'M CALLING DAD.

... WHEN IT STARTS TO RAIN, EVERYTHING'S THE SAME.

DISCONTENT MAKES RICH MEN POOR.

I'LL KEEP THAT IN MIND.

GIGGLE

GIGGLE

BYE, BEN!

HEY.

YOU WEREN'T AT SCHOOL TODAY.

I WASN'T FEELING WELL.

OH.

IS SHE OKAY?

I DUNNO.

I WAS WONDERING IF I COULD...

I WANNA REJOIN THE BAND.

OH, REALLY?

I WAS TALKING TO LUCY, NOT YOU.

MAYA DOESN'T EVEN LIKE SINGING, SO...

WHAT HAPPENED?

YOU *KNOW* WHAT HAPPENED...

SO ARE YOU MAKING CONNOR CHOOSE A SIDE?

SHH!

LOOK, I HEARD ABOUT THE SCOOTER THING.

I CAN JUST PAY YOU FOR IT, AND THEN MAYA CAN KEEP IT, AND WE CAN PUT ALL OF THIS BEHIND US.

JUST LIKE THAT.

...

WHAT'S IT WORTH TO YOU?

I HAVE FIFTY DOLLARS.

FINE.

AND YOU ALWAYS GET WHAT YOU WANT, DON'T YOU?

HONESTLY, MAYA WILL BE RELIEVED, BUT HOW'RE WE GONNA LEARN ANOTHER SONG IN LESS THAN TWO WEEKS?

HA.

BUT I'M NOT SINGING "TWIST AND SHOUT." I WANNA DO A DIFFERENT BEATLES SONG.

I'VE BEEN GOOGLING THIS STRESS FRACTURE THING. IT SEEMS LIKE THE PROGNOSIS IS GOOD. I MEAN, COMPARED TO A BROKEN HIP.

SHE'S ON BED REST FOR AT LEAST EIGHT WEEKS. SHE'S GONNA GO CRAZY.

YOUR DAD'S BUYING HER AN IPAD.

(SIGH) YEAH.

LUCY, MY BEING THERE WOULDN'T HELP. I'D JUST MAKE HER GO CRAZY FASTER.

YOU SHOULD'VE BEEN HERE THREE DAYS AGO! WE HAD TO CALL AN AMBULANCE AGAIN—IT WAS REALLY SCARY.

I'M SORRY.

I'M NOT COMING TO LONDON.

I CAN'T.

WHAT?

YOU JUST WANT ME TO GO AWAY SO YOU CAN HANG OUT WITH YOUR GIRLFRIEND.

LUCY?!

I HAVE WORK TO DO!

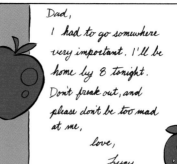

Dad,
I had to go somewhere very important. I'll be home by 8 tonight. Don't freak out, and please don't be too mad at me,
love,
Lucy

I NEED TO TALK TO JOHN.

JOHN?

JOHN LENNON.

!

I KNOW WHAT I'M DOING.

YEAH. RUNNING OFF TO TALK TO A DEAD MAN. WHERE ARE YOU REALLY GOING?

LUCY?

8:15 AM

NYC

...AND ANY TIME YOU FEEL THE PAIN, HEY JUDE, REFRAIN...

REMEMBER, BUNNYBEAR, DON'T EVER LET ANYONE STOP YOU FROM BEING WHO YOU ARE OR GOING WHERE YOU NEED TO GO.

I GAVE YOUR MOM THAT ADVICE YEARS AGO, AND I THINK MAYBE THAT WAS THE ONE TIME IN HER LIFE SHE EVER LISTENED TO ME.

TAKE ME TO CENTRAL PARK, PLEASE.

IT'S A BIG PARK, KID— YOU KNOW WHERE YOU WANT ME TO DROP YOU OR WHAT?

UM... STRAWBERRY FIELDS, THE MEMORIAL...

RIGHT.

276

10:37
DAD
I'M OK
DON'T WORRY

CLICK FLIP

THANKS.

A-

MOM?

I'VE BEEN EXPECTING YOU.

THE WORLD'S NEVER QUITE AS BIG AS YOU THINK IT IS.

HOW DID YOU...

VANESSA CALLED YOUR DAD, AND YOUR DAD CALLED ME IN A PANIC.

I DIDN'T TELL VANESSA WHERE...

"YOUR DAD, BEING YOUR DAD, PUT ALL THE CLUES TOGETHER."

WHERE ELSE WOULD YOU GO TO TALK TO JOHN LENNON?

YEAH, BUT HOW...

LUCKY ME, I WAS IN TOWN LAST NIGHT FOR A MEETING. I WAS GOING TO SURPRISE YOU AND COME FOR THE TALENT SHOW ON THURSDAY.

I LOVE YOU, LUCE.

KISS

YOU'RE AWFULLY QUIET.

I'M JUST REALLY AFRAID — OF EVERYTHING.

YOU GOT HERE ALL BY YOURSELF.

THAT TOOK SOME GUTS!

NO, I MEAN, THE TALENT SHOW —

WE DON'T HAVE ENOUGH TIME TO PRACTICE, AND COOKIE...

AND AFTER "HEY JUDE," THERE'S ONLY ONE MORE BEATLES ALBUM, AND THEN WHAT?

IT'S ALL OVER.

THE END.

SWEETHEART, **YOU ARE** ONLY JUST BEGINNING. EVERYTHING'S AHEAD OF YOU.

IMAGINE

YOU'LL ALWAYS HAVE COOKIE AND THE BEATLES — THE PEOPLE, THE MUSIC YOU LOVE, WILL BE INSIDE OF YOU, A PART OF WHO YOU ARE, FOREVER.

BUT...

YOU'RE GONNA BE JUST FINE, SWEETHEART. BELIEVE ME.

NOW, WE BETTER CALL YOUR DAD BEFORE HE MELTS INTO A PUDDLE OF WORRY.

CONNOR JUST BROKE UP WITH ME.

WHY?

HE BROKE UP WITH ME AND THEN WALKED TO WORK.

THIS MORNING BEFORE SCHOOL, HE SENT ME A RECOMPILED VERSION OF "LET IT BE," WITH, LIKE, OTHER TAKES AND EARLY RECORDINGS OF THE SONGS.

I'VE BEEN LISTENING TO IT, BUT I ...

HA.

"LET IT BE," LIKE THAT'S SO EASY. MAYBE FOR HIM.

HE'S A STUPID IDIOT!

NO, HE'S NOT!

I'M NEVER GONNA LOVE ANYBODY ELSE EVER, LUCY, I SWEAR.

SIGH

LOVE AND BE LOVED.

279

SAYS THE MAN WHO'S ALWAYS ALONE. WHO D'YOU LOVE?

HE LOVES EVERYONE IN THIS WHOLE TOWN. EVEN THE PEOPLE HE HASN'T MET.

DO YOU LOVE ME, OLD MAN?

STOP IT, VANESSA!

DON'T YELL AT ME RIGHT NOW!

IN CASE YOU'RE WONDERING, I'M FINE. NOTHING MUCH HAPPENING IN *MY LIFE*. I JUST WENT TO NEW YORK BY MYSELF, AND NOW I'M GROUNDED FOR SIX WEEKS. THANK YOU FOR TELLING ON ME, BY THE WAY!

WHATEVER. I PROBABLY SAVED YOUR LIFE.

WE'RE GONNA HAVE TO CHANGE OUR SONG FOR THE TALENT SHOW.

NO WAY. YOU JUST MADE EVERYONE LEARN—

I DON'T CARE! SINGING THAT SONG NOW IS LIKE STABBING MYSELF IN THE HEART!

ARE YOU KIDDING ME? THE SONG ISN'T ABOUT YOU! THE SHOW ISN'T, EITHER!

IT'S ABOUT THE BAND, AND WHEN WE PLAY, WHEN IT ACTUALLY WORKS, WE'RE MORE THAN OURSELVES, MORE THAN EVERYTHING, MORE THAN LOVE, EVEN...

LUCY, WAIT!

AND IN THE END, THE LOVE YOU TAKE IS EQUAL TO THE LOVE YOU MAKE.

BETSY ROSS
SCHOOL FOR
GIRLS
SPRING
TALENT
★ SHOW ★

WELCOME

GOOD LOVIN'... GOOD LOVIN'... GOOD LOVIN'!

TAP TAP TAP

TAP TAP

CLAP CLAP CLAP CL
CLAP CLAP CLAP
CLAP
CLAPCLAP CL

WE KINDLY ASK YOUR PATIENCE FOR A FEW MOMENTS AS OUR NEXT GROUP OF PERFORMERS MOVES THEIR EQUIPMENT INTO PLACE.

EXIT

AND NOW, GEORGIANNA BIRK, RUPA KHANNA, LUCY SUTCLIFFE, AND VANESSA TAKAHASHI ARE STRAWBERRY JAM!

CLAP CLAP CLAPCLAP CLAP CLAP CLAP CLAP

THIS IS A SONG YOU PROBABLY KNOW — IT'S BY JOHN, PAUL, GEORGE, AND RINGO.

OH MY GOD, I JUST RHYMED.

KLIK
KLAK

DON'T LET ME DOWN...

HEY, DON'T LET ME DOWN...

AH! DON'T LET ME DOWN.

CLAP CLAP CLAP
LAP CLAP CLAPC
CLAP

I'D LIKE TO SAY THANK YOU ON BEHALF OF THE GROUP AND MYSELF. IF WE COULD DO JUST ONE MORE...

?

CLAP CLAP CLAP
CLAP CLAP CLAP CLAP
CLAP CLAP

"DOORS AND WALLS."

BUT WE HAVEN'T...

WE CAN DO IT.

THIS IS A SONG YOU DEFINITELY DON'T KNOW, BECAUSE WE WROTE IT OURSELVES.

TIK TIK TIK TIK

DOORS AND WALLS, THEY ARE FOR FOOLS...

JUST ASK THE BEES - THEY DON'T FOLLOW RULES. I HEAR THIS BUZZING IN MY BRAIN...

I SAID I'D BABYSIT RYAN TONIGHT.

AGAIN.

FOR FREE.

YOU'RE A GOOD GIRL.

PAT PAT

I BETTER GET GOING.

SAY GOODBYE TO YOUR MOM.

I WILL.

KISS

I'M SO PROUD OF YOU, BUNNYBEAR.

YOUR MOM AND I HAVE WATCHED YOUR PERFORMANCE ON THAT I-GIZMO A DOZEN TIMES.

?!

WHAT'RE YOU DOING?

I'VE DECIDED TO STAY, JUST THROUGH THE SUMMER, WHILE HER HIP HEALS.

OH MY GOD! REALLY?!

Sigh

REALLY.

THIS IS GREAT!

WE'LL SEE.

YOU HAVEN'T TOLD COOKIE?

NOT YET.

THIS IS SO, SO GREAT.

I GOTTA GO.

LOVE YOU! BYE!

coda: summer

WILL YOU BE MY SANCTUARY, MY PLACE TO GO, MY SOMEONE WHO KNOWS...

THE NEW LYRICS SOUND GREAT. I'VE GOTTA THINK OF THE RIGHT CHORD TO END ON.

IT'S TOO HOT TO THINK.

YOU NEED SOME WATER?

WE GOTTA GET THIS SONG FIGURED OUT!

GEEZ. STRESS CASE!

YEAH, BECAUSE I ENTERED US IN THE BATTLE OF THE BANDS...

AT THE COUNTY FAIR? BUT THAT'S FOR REAL MUSICIANS!

WE'RE REAL MUSICIANS!

WAY TO GO, BOSS!

I TOLD MY MOM I'D GO SHOPPING WITH HER.

YEAH, MY MOM'S GONNA BE HERE ANY SEC...

SEE YOU GUYS TOMORROW.

SEE YA.

LATER ALLIGATORS!

BYE.

AFTERWORD

I was fourteen when John Lennon was murdered. I heard the news at school from a friend, who, knowing I was a huge Beatles fan, offered his sincere condolences. Of course, Lennon's death hit me hard, but looking back, it seems as if it didn't hit me quite as hard as it should have. Already, my musical interests were moving in other directions.

When I was very young, my dad had given me his Beatles albums and an old guitar from his college years, along with a book of guitar chords. It didn't take me long to learn a few chords and start to figure out some Beatles songs. Those albums were, more or less, the soundtrack to my childhood. By the time I reached high school, I knew all the songs by heart, both the big hits and the filler (if any Beatles songs can really be called filler). But by then, I had discovered punk rock, and new wave, and all those bands that were a part of the second British invasion of the 1980s. So, I put away my Beatles albums, for a while, as I joined my own band and tried to discover myself.

In my twenties, I began to rebuild my music collection on CD and rediscovered the Beatles, this time on the albums as they were originally released in the UK. I found I still knew the words to every song. It was like they were in my blood, an essential part of my being. Listening to them with mature ears, I appreciated the Beatles' genius and their ability to compose near-perfect pop songs.

My story is not so different from the millions of other people who feel that same connection to the Fab Four's music. It was not a surprise that I should meet and marry someone who shared my love for them. And, as my dad planted the seeds of my Beatlemania in me, Kiara's passion for the Beatles came through her dad, Bill.

In July of 2019, we took our then three-year-old daughter, Esmé, to see Paul McCartney. Grandpa Bill came with us. It was the first time both Esmé and I saw a Beatle. Over that past year, she and I had learned to sing and play the song "Blackbird," and when we realized it was part of Paul's set that night, we all turned to one another with looks of simultaneous recognition. This was heightened by the fact that this one perfect moment was happening in the midst of what had otherwise been a difficult year for us due to a health scare. There we were, three generations, equally enthralled and touched by this music, which was now fifty years old. I could not have imagined the same scene with my own grandfather.

Pop music today is no longer synonymous with rock 'n' roll, like it was when I was a kid. Guitar music has become a genre once more, no longer the mainstream. But there's still something special about getting together with a few friends in a garage, turning your instruments up loud, and working it out. Who knows if Esmé or her siblings will take up an instrument or join a band, but music is such a given in their lives. It is all around them. It is a natural presence for them. I can see it in the unselfconscious way they sing. And that is how it should be.

Music was clearly the lifeblood of the four lads from Liverpool as well. None of them knew any other professional life, and it's a bit crazy to consider that by the time they had reached the age of thirty, their careers as Beatles were over. When I was in my thirties myself, I sat down to watch the movie *Imagine*, about the life of John Lennon, and I finally broke down and cried like I felt I should have back in high school—both for John's death, and the fact that the Beatles were no more. But I also remember something John said about people mourning the Beatles—that if you still wanted to hear them, all you had to do was play their records. He said it in a way that was flip and slightly callous, and it was during a time when he was trying to demystify the Beatles, both for himself and others. But those records *are* a gift, greater than he was probably willing to admit, for millions of folks who have been touched by their deceptively simple genius, and for millions more still waiting to hear them and be inspired by them.

Albany, California

SOUNDTRACK

What follows is a list of songs, albums, and artists listened to, sung, or referred to in the story. The page number is indicated first, followed by artist, song, album, and label. Regarding Beatles songs—since Lucy is listening to her dad's old LPs, the American vinyl release of the song is listed first, followed by the UK release, and in a few cases, the current CD release.

Note: Fictional songs are marked with an asterisk.

1   *One 4 All, "I Love You More," *Strength in Numbers* (Brinki)
5   *One 4 All, "Together Forever," *One For All* (Brinki)
11 *One 4 All, "Say Goodbye, Baby," *The More the Merrier* (Brinki)
18 Pharoah Sanders, "Yemenja," *Journey to the One* (Theresa Records)
30 The Beatles, "I Saw Her Standing There," *Introducing the Beatles* (Veejay), *Meet the Beatles* (Capitol), *Please Please Me* (Parlophone)
33 The Beatles, "Misery," *Introducing the Beatles* (Veejay), *Please Please Me* (Parlophone)
36 "Castle on a Cloud," *Les Miserables*
36 *Miss Deed, "Do The Deed," *Do the Deed* (Brinki)
37 Carly Rae Jepsen, "Call Me Maybe," *Curiosity* (School Boy, Interscope)
38 The Beatles, "Till There Was You," *Meet the Beatles!* (Capitol), *With the Beatles* (Parlophone)
46 The Beatles, "It Won't Be Long," *Meet the Beatles!* (Capitol), *With the Beatles* (Parlophone)
51 John's Children, "Desdemona," UK single (Track)
52 Cat Power, *Sun* (Matador)
55 The Archies, "Sugar, Sugar," *Everything's Archie* (Calendar)
56 The Beach Boys, *Pet Sounds* (Capitol)
56 Gram Parsons, *Grievous Angel* (Reprise)
63 The Beatles, "Roll Over Beethoven," *The Beatles Second Album* (Capitol), *With the Beatles* (Parlophone)
74 Jimmie Davis and Charles Mitchell (authorship disputed) "You Are My Sunshine"
78 The Beatles, "A Hard Day's Night," *A Hard Day's Night* (Capital, Parlophone)
84 The Beatles, "Komm Gib Mir Deine Hand," *Something New* (Capitol), German single (Odeon Records), *Past Masters* (Apple, CD release)

ACKNOWLEDGMENTS

Over the past five years, as *Lucy in the Sky* has come together, our little family has grown into a big family. Pregnancy, childbirth, and life with babies and toddlers have sometimes slowed our writing and illustrating progress, so we would like to thank everyone involved with this book for their patience. More importantly, though, we would like to thank our children for allowing Mama and Dada the necessary time to work. Esmé, Arthur, and Julian, we love you more than words can say, more than there are stars in the sky, and even more than the Beatles.

It is hard to imagine where we would be without our steadfast agent, Alice Tasman, who first suggested we try our hand at a middle grade book. Also, many, many thanks to everyone at First Second, especially Calista Brill, Robyn Chapman, Kirk Benshoff, and Molly Johanson for their enthusiasm and dedication to *Lucy*.

We are forever grateful to our own parents for their love and support, and, of course, for raising us with the Beatles. Bill Brinkman (aka Popsie), you are the most loving "manny" in the world—we couldn't have finished this book without you!

Our Waldorf community has supported us with encouragement, kindness, childcare, and delicious meals. Sharon Lacay, you are an inspiration!

Finally, thank you to our dear friends Augusta Meill, Alyson Brown, Jeremy Greco, Andy Peters, and the good people (past and present) at the Booksmith in San Francisco, including you, Aileen Long.

FRIENDS! MUSIC! MYSTERIES!
These great graphic novels have it all!

BE PREPARED
by Vera Brosgol

Come along with Vera as she goes to summer camp for the first time ever!

STARGAZING
by Jen Wang

Meet Christine and Moon, two friends who have a lot in common, but who couldn't be more different!

JUKEBOX
by Nidhi Chanani

Fly through music history with Shaheen and Tannaz in this time-traveling adventure!

CICI'S JOURNAL
by Joris Chamblain and Aurélie Nyret

Join Cici as she explores the secrets and mysteries hidden in her hometown!

Great graphic novels for every reader